# da word

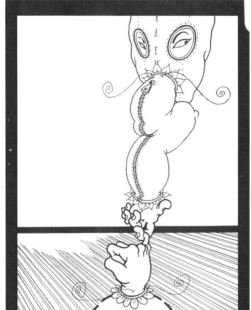

## Lee A. Tonouchi

Bamboo Ridge Press
2001

ISBN 0-910043-61-2
This is issue #78 of *Bamboo Ridge, Journal of Hawai'i Literature and Arts*
(ISSN 0733-0308).
Copyright © 2001 Bamboo Ridge Press
Published by Bamboo Ridge Press
Indexed in the American Humanities Index
Bamboo Ridge Press is a member of the Council of Literary Magazines
and Presses (CLMP).

Artwork: Ryan Higa
Typesetting and design: Wayne Kawamoto
Consultant on Odo orthography in "Pijin Wawrz": Kent Sakoda


Bamboo Ridge Press is a nonprofit, tax-exempt corporation formed in 1978 to foster the appreciation, understanding, and creation of literary, visual, or performing arts by, for, or about Hawaii's people. This project is supported in part by grants from the National Endowment for the Arts (NEA), the Hawai'i Community Foundation, and the State Foundation on Culture and the Arts (SFCA) celebrating over thirty years of culture and the arts in Hawai'i. The SFCA is funded by appropriations from the Hawai'i State Legislature and by grants from the NEA.


*Bamboo Ridge* is published twice a year. For subscription information, back issues, or a catalog please contact:


Bamboo Ridge Press
P. O. Box 61781
Honolulu, HI 96839-1781
(808) 626-1481
brinfo@bambooridge.com
www.bambooridge.com


9 8 7 6 5 4 3 2                    01 02 03 04 05 06 07 08

Much mahalos to da following periodicals and anthologies wea some of da pieces insai dis collection wuz previously published—*The Asian Pacific American Journal, Bamboo Ridge: 20th Anniversary Issue, Bamboo Ridge: Journal of Hawai'i Literature and Arts, The Best of Honolulu Fiction: Stories from the Honolulu Magazine Fiction Contest, Chain, Growing Up Local: an anthology of poetry and prose from Hawai'i, The Hawai'i Review, Hawai'i Review: The Hawai'i Issue, Honolulu Magazine, Tinfish,* and *ZYZZYVA.*

## Artwork by Ryan Higa

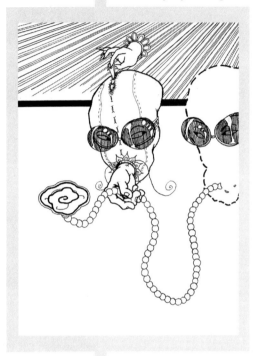

*Cover:* "prrrmk", 2000, acrylic on wood, 12"x12"
*Back cover:* "kppltt", 2000, acrylic on wood, 12"x12"
*Page one:* "hwht", 2000, ink on paper, 9"x12"
*Page four:* "fsssst", 2000, ink on paper, 9"x12"

Dis book iz dedi-K-ted 2 my N-spiration—
Tracie, U my material girl. Hi Inkie. Alwayz
tinking of U—Grammy guyz, Auntie J,
Papa Smurf, & MOM. Shout-out 2 my
co-konspiratorz & konfidantz—
da HYBOLICS Krew—Monkey Girl &
Longshot. Wea would I-B witout my
thera-P group—Da Pidgin Queen,
Darth Koza, Scott Masaki, Pu-Man, J, &
Catwoman. UR2KOOL2B4GOT10. 4 planny
of my storiez I wen borrow your name k
Aaron, no werry U can hav 'em back.
Tanx 2 Mr. Willlllllson 4 showin' me my
first PGN poem. N-4 C-ing dis ting thru
tanx yea, Happy Happy Joy Joy, X-Man,
G, Wayne No Name, & U-2-O-FUTS.

# da word

Back den I nevah know. I wuz only one six grader trying fo' make 'em into Punahou, 'Iolani, or Kamehameha. My faddah wanted me fo' get in. I dunno why. Friggin' expensive go private school. I nevah like go cuz pressure ah. Get dat debt dat I gotta repay my faddah now. Not only I gotta be grateful fo' him working hod, taking care me aftah my mom wen divorce us, but now I gotta be tankful dat he sending me to one "good" school so I can go "mainland" college and come one doctor. And not just anykine mainland school, but da kine "good" kine mainland school, preferably one of da Ivory league kine schools. So to him I'm jus like one investment. He nevah axed me if I wanted fo' go private school. I guess wuz jus so he could brag to our family and all his friends, but wot about my friends?

Laurie wuz my friend, not by choice, more by default. She came our school from Oregon fourt' grade time. Since den da teachers always put us together in da smaht group. I mostly only talked to her in class, recess time I cruised wit my friends. We got along pretty good, except fo' da fack dat she wuz competetive, dat wuz one of her idiosyncrasies. Das my new word I wen learn. Da teacher wen make us learn one new word everyday and we gotta make one coconut-shape ornament and stick 'em on da Vocabulary Tree. Good fun wuz learning words. One time I called Laurie "demented" and she had to go look 'em up before she could give me her rebuttal, *"I'm not a person suffering from dementia or the irreversible deterioration of mental faculties. I'm not like stupid you know."* Yeah, right. Wotevahs. One noddah time I wen trick her li'dat wen I sed, "Ho Laurie, why you always gotta look so pulchritudinous, ah?" Ho, dat set her off. She nevah know wot dat meant, but she kept arguing, arguing wit me until finally she found out dat it meant beautiful and den wuz all like wop your jaws[1] ah. Some people, cannot take one compliment I tell you boy.

[1] *facial disgracial*

Of all da people I wuz going miss, Laurie wuzn't one of 'em. Chances wuz dat I wuz going be seeing a whole lot more of her though cuz she sed she wuz going private school too. None of her friends back in Portland wuz in private schools she sed. She wuz happy dat she wuz special. I guess I wanted fo' get in cuz I nevah like be lacking ah, but still I nevah like all my friends tink I wuz high nose li'dat. At least Laurie nevah have to worry about her rep cuz she had dat himakas[2] ting going down fo' long time already. Plenny people nevah like Laurie. Da girls nevah like her cuz she wuz pretty and she knew dat she wuz pretty. And she had dat "I'm one intellectual" kine attitude ah. She wuz da one always raising her hand in class, fully brown nosing, trying fo' be teacher's pet.

[2] *tantaran*

One day da teacher wuz going over everybody's essays on how wuz their summer vacation. He wuz really picking on Mits Funai and Barry Santos and he made dem go up in front da class and read their essays. Could tell he had problems wit Barry's body surfing at Point Panic papah. Teach sed he used to surf there too wen he wuz growing up so I nevah catch why he wuz geeving dem da business. At first I tot da problem wuz dat da essay wuz all "fiction" ah, cuz Barry, him, he talk da talk, but he no walk da walk ah, you know da kine. Him, he pressure out wen his head stay undah water li'dat. Ninety feet and glassy. I no tink so. But wuzn't so much da content, but da manner in which Barry wen go write 'em.

*"Barry, how many times must I tell you? You musn't write like how you speak."*

"Hah?!" Barry's head jerked back.

*"Who can tell the class what is wrong with Barry's writing?"*

"Oh, Barry, he da kine. He stay abundantly writing in one freestyle kine manner using, I mean utilizing, large quantities of informal neologisms, ah?" Mits attempted trying fo' incorporate as many of da new coconut-kine vocabulary words as he could remembah into dat one response.

*"The problem is that both Barry AND Mits use too many colloquialisms,"* Laurie volunteered, dis time witout raising her hand.

"Try like, das not wot I sed?" Mits whispered into my ear.

"I tink so, but maybe wuz too wordy or someting ah."

*"That was an excellent response Laurie. You speak very well."*

"Yeah Laurie, you talk sooo gooood," Fay added sarcastically.

*"Laurie speaks WELL,"* da teacher correck-ed in his stern voice, silencing da snickering of da class as he banged da yardstick on da table. Talks good, speaks well. Same diffs. So long you get da idea. Laurie wuz fully irking today. Couldn't wait till recess fo' play tetherball wit da gang.


Usually Laurie stayed in class during recess time. I tink so she sked da sun or someting, ass why she so white. I dunno wot she doing in da classroom. Probably kissing up to da teacher sa'more. Probably erasing da blackboard or straightening da desks or someting. Ass why all of us wen stare wen Laurie started walking toward da tetherball pole.

"No mo' caboose k," Barry sed, making like normal.

"Get swing?" Fay and Bernard wen ax.

"Ne'mine da rules, jus play already befo' we gotta go back class," I sed anxiously as I saw Laurie smiling at me.

*"Hi, what are you guys doing?"* Laurie axed as she stood on da outside of da concrete circle twirling her long black hair round and round wit her fingers.

"Wot YOU doing? You no belong hea, girlie. Jus go back wea you came from," Fay hollered.

Wuz so unexpecked wot Laurie's reaction wuz. I would've tot dat she would've jus make like one BANANA and split ah, make like one drum and beat it, jus make like one shovel and DIG li'dat, but instead she wen jus sit down and cry. Barry and da boyz wen go leave fo' go play on one noddah pole. I wanted fo' go have fun too, but I felt sorry ah fo' Laurie. Torn. Dat love-hate deals.

"Laurie, no cry," I sed hoping she would stop fass so I could go join my friends.

*"Why . . ."* She sed sniffling, her eyes coming all red.

"Come den, we go walk around befo' people tink wuz me who wen make you cry."

I helped her up and we moved from da grassy area to walking along da lanai. I got her paper towels from da bachroom so she could wipe her face. We walked togethers fo' a while, our shoulders brushing occasionally.

My body came all stiff li'dat wen witout looking at me she jus locked her left pinky wit my right pinky as our arms swung together in unison. I made one strange face making quick kine side eyes, getting ready fo' make da break if in case had anybody looking ah.

My eyes stopped scanning and focused in on her wen I noticed dat she wuz humming one song.

"Wot song is dat?"

*"It's from* Westside Story.*"*

"Oh."

*"The musical.* Westside Story. *They made it into a movie. It's based on Shakespeare's* Romeo and Juliet. *You don't know it? How can you not know it? It's a classic."*

"Oh. So . . ." I sed, not knowing wot else fo' say as I noticed dat we wuz all da way in da front of campus, by da office already. "So, uh, we go head back li'dat befo' da bell ring ah, you know da kine."

*"Why do you talk funny sometimes?"*

"Hah?! You saying I should be one comedian?"

*"Not funny, humorous, but funny, strange."*

"Oh."

And den there wuz silence again as we continued walking back. We nevah talk until we wuz passing da libary wen Laurie wen ax, *"So when are you going to call to set up an appointment for your interview at Punahou?"*

"Ah, I do 'em bumbye," I sed casual kine, not really wanting to tink about it at da moment.

*"When?"* Laurie sed, wrinkling her eyebrows together.

"Bumbye."

*"What's that, BUMBYE?"*

"Bumbye. Bum . . . bye," I repeated slowly.

*"Like ye-ah. That's not a word. You're making it up."*

"It is too one word."

*"I'll bet you it's not!"*

Laurie wuz starting to piss me off. See, dat love-hate deals. Attractive, but get attitude. Since we wuz by da libary she sed we should go check da dictionary cuz das wea dey had da big humangoso dictionary. Laurie wuz so confident dat she wuz right dat she even bet me dat whoever loss would have to carry da winner's books fo' a week while walking in between classes. I nevah like dat bet cuz to me ees like either way she win cuz I nevah like people tink dat she wuz my girlfriend or noting. So I toll her if I won den she had fo' buy me one extra milk fo' lunch. Only ten cents, but ees not da money, but mo' pride ah. Cuz I knew I wuz right. We walked into da libary and went to da stand wit da big American Heritage Dictionary, Unabridged Edition. Friggin' ukubillion[3] pages insai. My word garans going be insai there I tot, tinking of how sweet dat milk wuz going taste. I flipped through da pages wit Laurie friggin' tip-toeing and staring over my shoulders so she could be da first one NOT fo' see da word. Bumbye. As I flipped to da B's my mind wandered as I tot—das one word ah? Bumbye. Simple word too. Hakum Laurie dunno 'em? Nah, nah, no doubt. Laurie going be da one who lose out. Bumbye gotta be one word, I heard my Grandma use 'em sooo many times. "Grandma, wen you going take me Disneyland?" "Bumbye." So bumbye can mean later on, indefinite kine, possibly nevah. Or "Grandma, hakum you no always flush da toilet aftah you pau shi shi?" "Cuz bumbye pohō water." So bumbye is also like consequently or as one result kine. See, so das two definitions already. So hakum dis friggin' diction-ary no' mo da word, I tot as I saw one smile begin to form on Laurie's lips. Maybe I stay spelling 'em wrong? B-U-M . . . B-Y-E. Das right ah? Maybe ees B-U-M-B-A-I? Or B-U-M-B-Y? I flipped frantically look-ing fo' da kine alternative spellings. I kept flipping back and forth, back and forth, making sure fo' dou-ble check each one. But nevah have none of da spellings. Bumbye wuzn't one word.

I quickly looked fo' da meejum size Webster's dictionary, cuz da big one had so many words dat ees possible fo' miss dat one

[3] *choke*

word ah. But even da kine Webster's nevah get 'em. I wen check wot year da dictionaries wuz. If wuz old maybe I could get off on one technicality. Laurie wuz all jumping up and down, squealing small kine. Finally I ran to da librarian's desk and axed fo' borrow her little Random House pocket-size dictionary. Even though dat one wuz smaller, had all da important, high frequency, coconut-kine garans ball barans going be on da test kine words ah, so I figured gotta have 'em in dat one cuz ees pretty common ah, but still nevah get 'em.

I held da small dictionary open not knowing wot fo' do. Da bell rang as Laurie turned and grabbed my arm fo' lead me back to class. I cradled da dictionary snug in my right hand as she pulled my oddah arm sa'more and slid her hand down to hold my hand. I let her fingertips slip through mine as she looked back once and den turned to leave toward da double doors. "Bumbye" wuzn't one coconut-kine word. I stood, still looking at da dictionary in my palm, part of me wanting to memorize every single friggin' word in there, part of me wanting to friggin' throw it at Laurie's head before she left, jus to hear wot kinda noise it would make.

*Finished*

We wuz da proud Nā Ali'i. Da proud warriors of 'Aiea High School. We wuz new to da school, but me and James had plans fo' rule. K, maybe we nevah have to rule necessarily, but at least kick ass. Wuz one time of definition. Wuz one time fo' form our new identities. We nevah like be squares like, well I no like

**square** mention any names cuz das mean ah, but you can pretty much tell who's cool and who's a dork ah. We wuz freshmen—old intermediate school boys reborn as new high school fresh-men. Men wit big time dreams. James had big hopes of impressing dis girl from Guam, Laressa Dimalanta. He joined cross country jus so he could try hook up wit her. Me, since intermediate, I had one crush on Joy, but I wuzn't about fo' join da cheerleading squad jus so I could be wit her. Although technically wuz possible cuz had dis one guy on da squad, but everyone tot he wuz a fag. Anyhow wuzn't one verbal agreement, but me and James always had dis rivalry goin' on. Wenevah I did someting, he had fo' do me one bettah. Da battle raged on throughout our freshman year, wit neither guy gaining da true upperhand.

Life is one battle, kinda like one wrestling match. Like Mr. Fuji who wen trow Don Muraco da cane fo' whack Ricky "The Dragon" Steamboat. He may have won dat particular match, but I remember in one of their later re-matches Fuji did da same ting, only dis time Steamboat wen catch da cane and use 'em on Muraco wen da ref wuzn't looking. See, everybody get bachi. Like wen someting bad happen to somebody my ma says, "If you cannot say anything nice about somebody, then don't say anything at all." I guess I nevah listen so good fo' dat lecture cuz one time she wen go trip so I wen laugh. Anyway, not five minutes later I wen trip too. Das Bachi. Wot goes around comes around, ass how da saying goes. Cosmic karma. Da eternal workings of da universe. Like one perpetual nevah ending struggle.

At 'Aiea, James and I grappled in our own little feud. I joined da cross country team too, not jus cuz James joined, but cuz I wuz kinda hoping dat Joy would do some cheers fo' us li'dat. But I found out dey only cheered fo' da real teams like football and stuff. Fo' awhile I considered joining da football team too. I wuz in weight training wit "Fatu" and "Samu," Da Samoan Swat Team, and dey toll me try out. Dem, dey wuz vicious, their motto wuz "Ees one bad game if we don't maim." Dey tried showing me some of their moves li'dat, so maybe I could impress da coach next year at try-outs. I gritted my teet and tried my bess fo' be one lean-mean-tackling machine. Eventually I managed to get da cleverly appropriate nickname, "Stickman." Unfortunately wuzn't cuz I played football too rough. Dey sed wuz cuz I wuz too skinny and my tackles wuzn't quite effective li'dat. Anyhow, befo' too much people got hurt, I decided fo' quit. Eh, ees possible people could trip and fall ovah my prone body dat stay all hurtin' on da ground.

Da first time I got James good wuz wen we wuz running on Maui and I sed, "Look James, Laressa catching up." Den he turned fo' look behind and he crashed into one tree. We came in lass dat race. Laressa nevah see James actually hitting da tree, but she did come around later and see him all comatose on da ground. Pretty big wuz da bruise. No ax him about it ah. He's pretty touchy. Aftah all, ees a pretty sore subject. Ha ha ha ha. K, not funny.

He got me back good wen we wuz in Mr. Hirata's math class. Joy wuz in our class too. Sometimes I tried fo' ack smaht in class fo' impress Joy. But hod fo' balance 'em cuz you no like make TOO smaht, cuz bumbye you goin' be teacher's pet or one nerd. So I used to only answer wen nobody else knew 'em. Well actually, wen nobody else knew 'em, I usually nevah know 'em too, but James he smaht math ah, so he used to slip me da answers li'dat. Dat wuz pretty cool of him.

So wuz kinda unexpected wen one day we wuz cruising in da room during recess. Joy wuz axing Mr. Hirata fo' help on one problem. James and me wuz cruising nearby. Das wen James sed, "Aaron, we go play Portagee Arm Wrestle." Wot's dat, I tot. So I sed, "How you play dat?" "Make like you flexing you bicep," he sed. So I did. I tink Joy wuz looking, but I wuzn't sure. Big ah my arm. She bettah have been looking. All my hours invested wit my Hulkamania workout set from Kay-Bee. You looking or wot Joy? Come closer and see. Come closer. Look at da largest pythons in da world. Da 15" guns. Come closer and look at my arms. Come closer to me. See mo' big ah come, wen you come mo' close. Perspective li'dat. Learn dat in art class. Anyhow, so I wen put my flexed arm on da table and James wen put his elbow opposite me and he wen go stick his hand on top my fist. He sed da object wuz I gotta pull toward me and he gotta try holl me back. Ho, dis goin' be so simple simon. Easy as 3.14. You get it? 3.14? Easy as Pi. K, dumb math joke. I coming one friggin' geek already.

Anyway, dis wuz my chance fo' show Joy I not only smaht, but beneath dis puny exterior lurks one physical powerhouse you know. So there I wuz pulling towards wit all my might. Small kine strain. I heard Mr. Hirata in da back, "Look those two guys." So I knew Joy wuz looking at me. If I could beat James in Portagee Arm Wrestle den surely I'd win her heart. Ho, is dat a bird I hear? No, mus be jus Joy's heart fluttering. My muscles tensed as I could sense James weakening. Den all of a sudden he released his hand from my fist. As a result, my fist wen fly and full-on hit my forehead. Mr. Hirata and Joy laughed. I put my head down on da desk and hid my head in shame. "I goin' get you sucka," I tot.

And da next week I got 'em back. James wore his white corduroy pants dat day to school. I teased him da whole day as I sang da Mr. Clean song. He wore his white cords specific cuz he heard dat Laressa tot white pants wuz sexy. So we wuz walking down to lunch. Usually we cruise wit Laressa and some oddah cross country guys at da cafe too. Today we wuz late though cuz Mr. Hirata nevah let us go till everybody turned in their tests. Anyhow so instead of walking down da sidewalk me and James wen cut thru and make shortcut down da grassy hill. And I dunno how it happened, but some-how, in da rush, our legs got all tangle and I acciden-tally tripped James somehow, and he kinda like, uh fell down and his white corduroy pants wuz now all green and white. He nevah like go eat anymo', but I toll 'em, "Nah only can see leedle bit. Not so bad. Plus, green and white, school spirit ah?" Well had some brown too, but I nevah like point dat out.

From den, James stopped giving me da answers in Mr. Hirata's class so I guess Joy must've been tinking I wuz slacking or someting, cuz I wuz getting loss wit da ress of da guys in geometry. I wuzn't da hottest wen came to math and neither wuz Joy. She wen in every recess fo' ax Mr. Hirata fo' help. Finally, I tink he got tired helping her so he wen get Dae Hwan Kim fo' tutor her. I tink wuz cuz he wanted time fo' eat his lunch during lunch time. Anyway, Dae Hwan wuz da Math Club vice president. Fo' weeks I saw dem together during both morning and lunch recess. Goin' over all da different postulates and theorems. Eventually wen Math Team competition time came, Dae Hwan nevah get time anymo' fo' help Joy so she wuz back to seeing Mr. Hirata. Mr. Hirata sed dat fo' da midterm everybody should try their bess and he would try get some of us either involved wit tutoring, Math Club, or maybe even part of da Math Team. I nevah like join Math Team. Buncha geeks. But I knew dat if I did good, den maybe Mr. Hirata would ax ME fo' help Joy. So I studied my butt off man. I nevah go Fun Factree fo' like two weeks so I could study. I knew I had fo' shoot fo' da highest cuz naturally Mr. Hirata goin' ax da highest guy.

Usually James get da highest score so I knew wuz goin' be hod fo' beat him. I knew he wuz still salty from da time I wen go accidentally make him fall down ah. So wuz da day of da test and I wuz focused. I only took my eyes off da papah only once fo' check da time. I tink plenny guys wuz mad at me cuz I took da longest so we had fo' wait five minutes extra befo' anybody could go lunch. I wanted fo' make sure all my answers wuz correck. We got our scores back da next class. I managed to beat James by two points. First time I evah beat James on one math test. While we wuz all doing problems in da book, Mr. Hirata wen call me ovah to his desk. I had one idea wot he wuz goin' ax me fo' do. I looked at Joy and I knew dis wuz goin' be da moment. But unfortunately da moment wuzn't as special as I tot wuz goin' be. Wuz da moment dat Mr. Hirata would nominate me fo' be one of da Math Team captains cuz one of da positions wuz vacated. I nevah like be captain I sed. I heard James snickering in da back. I found out later dat Dae Hwan wen quit da Math Team cuz da meets conflicted wit his Interact Club convention. So he went back to devoting his daily recesses to "interacking" wit my Joy. Fate can be cruel yeah.

Fate wuz cruel wen my grandfaddah had one stroke. He wen to da hospital fo' long time. Plenny people came visit and brought flowers and envelopes. Plenny people I nevah saw befo' even. Das wen I saw my grandma's black composition book ledger. She sed you always gotta write how much money people give fo' dis kine stuffs. She sed gotta keep track so wen your turn fo' give you can give back da same amount. Wot's da sense den yeah if you not goin' make profit. Wot's da sense if everybody goin' end up being "Even Steven." Goin' be like one Communist government. Mo' bettah everybody jus no give nobody noting already.

James nevah do noting, but he did laugh at me. And well, I tink I would've been mo' mad if James wuz da one who wuz tutoring

Joy again. Not like he liked Joy. He respecked da fack dat I liked her. I give 'em dat much. But not like he wuz exactly doing his bess fo' help me out either. He did withold vital information. He knew a few days befo' da test, dat Dae Hwan wuz tutoring Joy, but he wuz sandbagging there. Dirty ah. So I had fo' get 'em back. Fo' da homecoming pep rally, Jeaneen, da class president, wen ax me fo' do one skit or someting in front da whole freshman class. Dis is one good opportunity I tot. I wuz always interested in music. I couldn't play anyting, but I could sing not bad. I axed James if he wanted fo' go up wit me. He sed nah, shame. James wuz in band ah, so I figured maybe he would have suggestions on wot song fo' sing. I wanted fo' sing one Guns N' Roses song or someting, but hod ah wen no mo' music.

James gave me some of his music sheets from band fo' get ideas. Ass wen I saw 'em, "Puff The Magic Dragon." I dunno why, but I liked Puff The Magic Dragon, k. So I wen home dat night and wuz practicing. But as I wuz practicing I wuz tinking dis kinda lame. I mean dumb ah dis song? Like why is he all frolicking? Maybe I go change da words and make da kine Weird Al Yankovic den people goin' laugh ah. So I made my own song called "James Da Perfeck Student." Same tune, but change da lyrics. It went "James da perfeck student, get's A's on every test. Which is why in math and in science too, he's considered to be da bess. He's not satisfied, wit jus getting a pass. He's gotta beat everyone, in da whole gosh darn class." Anyhow I wuz tinking of making 'em "James LUM, Da Perfeck Student," but I nevah like make totally obvious wuz him ah. Had couple Jameses in our class. I couldn't wait fo' see his reaction.

Anyhow, aftah da pep rally I wen fo' look fo' James. Usually he cruise in Mr. Hirata's room. I wanted fo' rag him. Funny ah wuz. I walked insai and wen he saw me he gave me da stinkest look I evah saw. I tot we wuz only pretending kine, so I gave 'em one dirty look back.

"James, so wot you tot?" I axed.

He nevah say nahting and he jus played along sa'more, pretending fo' be mad and went out da oddah door. I followed him as he walked faster. And faster. And faster. I followed him until I came to one door, face to face wit one sign dat sed "Band Students Only."

James knew I couldn't go insai, so I jus sat down outside da door. I dunno why he wuz staying in da band room fo' so long. Bumbye people going tink he one band geek. I mean c'mon, cruising wit dem goin' only ruin his rep. He goin' be one social square if he no come out presoon. Maybe I should've signed up fo' band, but not like dey offer any cool instruments like electric guitar or bass. Like, I no tink I could ever be one member of Winger, Britney Fox, or Def Leppard playing da flute or da trumpet. Befo' time I could play da tonette. I should've argued dat da tonette should be included as one symphony instrument. But I guess cuz made of plastic, not brass, so ass why cannot ah.

I glanced at my watch as I wondered gee, why he taking so long? Five more minutes. He no can be mad fo' real kine ah? Good ah, I called him smaht? Why, mo' bettah I write one song "James da Stupid Dumbass No Can Take One Joke Student?" I no tink so yeah? Gee, some guys cannot take one compliment. In fack, he should've tanked me.

Wuzn't mean ah, wot I did? I wondah if Laressa going be all sympathetic wit him or wot? Wot if she get everybody on da cross country team fo' ice me out? Wot if nobody run practice wit me? I can jus imagine her not letting me go along wit everybody wen her maddah comes fo' pick her up aftah practice fo' go 7-Eleven eat Slurpee. Ah, no mattah. I like Icee bettah anyway. I guess I can jus wait fo' my faddah come get me by da back gate.

My faddah always watched da news. Wuz da years of da U.S. and da Soviet Union guys in da nuclear arms race. Wuz one dumb race actually. My faddah wuz all fo' building mo' missles. He sed cannot let da Soviets surpass us. Gotta support Reagan and be patriotic. I tot dis wuz dumb cuz if da Russians launch den we goin' launch den goin' jus keep goin' back and forth until da Earth is jus one big radioactive mushroom cloud. Like *The Day After.*

Sitting outside da bandroom, das how I felt, like I wuz da lass man on Earth aftah da nuclear holocaust. I'll give James five more minutes I tot, as I wen bring my knees in close and wrap my arms around. Might be I going be pre- much alone fo' most of dis semester. Because of me, James and Laressa probably going hook up I tink. I going be da common enemy dat brings dem togeth- er. She going haff to console him and put evil tots about me insai his head. Ees like me and her wuz all pulling apart wit James' arms. Den she wins da tug- of-war and walks off hand in hand wit James while I stay stuck behind.

Five more minutes. No time limit draws and no double disqualifications. I rested my head down on my knees as I reassured myself dat we wuzn't going go down to da time limit. Get plenny more time befo' time limit expires and da bell rings. I knew James wuz insai cooling down and plotting his revenge. I know he not going trow one fireball at me or whack me wit one chair,

*24*

but still, he gotta do someting. Wuz his turn get me back. I mean dis wuzn't how supposed to end. I tot all goin' come down to one climactic battle. One war between heaven and hell. "Da Incredible" Hulk Hogan vs. "Hot Rod" Rowdy Roddy Piper. Wrestlemania Showdown—Da War to Settle da Score. In da end goin' come down to one winner and one loser. Only I guess sometimes ees jus not quite clear which is which.

Everytime I went my Grandma's house she always gave me da same lecture. Wuz Valentine's Day so I went fo' visit her, drop off candy li'dat. Plus I had fo' drop off da orchid my Ma guys bought cuz her and Pa wuz going Pearl City Tavern fo' dinner. Usually my Faddah no let me drive all way townside, but so long as I came back befo' dahk, he sed can. Naturally Grandma wuz all happy fo' see me. I walked down da driveway, waved both hands in da air, and yelled

# *where to put your hands*

"Grandma!" so she knew dat I wuz coming. She looked through da kitchen jalousies and she sed, "Is dat you, Aaron?" She opened da screen door and I dunno why, but wen I handed her da stuffs her hands wuz acking all shaky ah. At first I tot maybe wuz cold, but actually wen I walked into da house wuz kinda hot. Ever since dey wen cut down da mango tree da house always come hot now. Today da house wuz supah stuffy too so I toll her I wuz going open some windows li'dat, but she sed, "No. Mo' bettah leave 'em close, bumbye people can see inside." I tot dat wuz strange cuz she always grumble wen we go my oddah Grandma's house dat their house no mo' air, but I nevah say noting. And da house wuz kinda quiet too today. Usually da TV stay on or my Grandpa stay listening to his Japanese radio station. Strange dat my Grandpa nevah say noting today too. Usually wen I come I yell "Hi Grandpa," too, but I tink he wuz sleeping cuz I nevah hear him yell, "Eh, who dat come!?"

My Grandma tanked me fo' da candy and she toll me tell my Ma guys tanks too. She wanted me fo' hug her ah, but I nevah like. Embarassing. I nevah hug her since small keed time. Feel weird hugging people. I dunno muss be a teenage guy ting I guess. Gotta be macho ah. So I jus did da fass kine pat pat on da shoulder. My Grandma axed me if I wanted to stay fo' dinner. I toll her "Okay, but I gotta eat early." I wuz kinda hoping she would offer, cuz oddahwise I would have to go home cook myself one Tyson Turkey TV Dinner. Last time I wen cook dat, my friend wen call and I forgot about 'em and came all ko-ge.

Anyway, soon as I came my Grandma wuz giving me da lecture about how I gotta fine one good kine wife who going take care me. Wife? I tot. Gee Grandma, I gotta kinda get girlfriend first, try like. She wuz all "Hakum you no mo' date tonight?" "Cuz Grandma, I gotta find da right girl. I no like choose any kine girl you know." Das wot I sed, but da troot wuz, I wuz too sked most of da time fo' talk to girls.

Since intermediate school time, I wuz sked fo' talk to Joy. She wuz like my ideal. Since Intermediate I always had her in at least one class. I wuzn't sure wot she wuz really. Maybe little bit Japanese, Hawaiian, Filipino, and maybe little bit Haole too. Wotevah she wuz, she looked full on Local. So Local dat fo' da second straight year, she wuz May Day Queen. I dunno why, but every time I wanted fo' talk to her I got all nerjous. And I came all sweaty too. So I figured da bes way not fo' get all anxiety attack is jus not fo' talk to her. Joy wuz pretty smart. She always scored high on tests and stuff, but I wouldn't say she wuz a nerd or nothing. Cuz one pretty nerd is like one contradiction in terms ah. So mentally she wuz up there. And ho physically she wuz pretty uh . . . developed fo' one sophomore. But you know wot wuz da one ting dat impressed me da most—she wuz always supah friendly. Even though me and her, we nevah had one conversation dat lasted mo' than couple minutes and not like we evah did anyting outside of class, but she still always sed hi to me wen we passed by in between classes. And not jus "Hi" and pau, but da kine "Hi" and da wave. And not one quick wave too, but da kine wave within da wave, where all her fingers stay up, den slowly starting from da pinky dey go down, until at last da index finger goes down, and den she do 'em one mo' time. Take like tree times as long as one regular wave, her patented Five Finger Linger Wave. Ees like she wanted fo' make sure dat everybody saw dat SHE wuz waving at ME.

My Grandma always sed, "Anykine girl you choose, me no like. Make sure you no marry Pōpolo girl now. Grandpa no like blacks. And no can be Filipino. My friend son from Lanakila go marry Filipino; now they divorce. Only two months you know. And no can be Chinee. Remembah your Uncle Richard, look he marry Chinee and look she take all his money and go leave him fo' marry Haole man. Japanee maybe, but depen on da family."

My Grandma so choosy. Going be one miracle if I evah do fine da right

28

girl. Usally wen my Grandma give me da lecture I jus zone li'dat until she pau. Sometimes I tink in my head—but not like everybody pure someting li'dat. Take Joy fo' example. She all kapakahi. Jus by looking, you dunno wot she is. And not jus her ah, I mean plenny people hapa ah. So sometimes I felt like saying, "Oh but Grandma, wot if she half Japanese, half Haole, and half Hawaiian?" I nevah like get into all da wot-if scenarios so wen my Grandma wuz pau and went into da kitchen I decided fo' cruise in da living room watch little bit WWF wrestling. Sometimes my Grandpa watch WWF wit me cuz almost like his sumo. I wuz going ax him if he wanted fo' watch, but ah I figgah he sleeping ah. Plus, I wuz kinda zoning ah, not really into da matches. Usually my Grandma's girl lecture no boddah me, but today wuz Valentine's and I wuz hoping I wuz going get one in da mailbox wen I went home. I wuz kinda worried.

Cuz wuz jus dis pass week I went to da Leo Club dance in da school cafeteria and I wen dance mostly wit da girls who wen ax me. Eh, I not ugly k if das wot you tinking. Had some girls wen ax me. I remembah I wanted so bad fo' dance wit Joy. I nevah like ax her cuz I admit, I wuz too chicken. I remembah da cafe wuz so crowded. I wuz getting so hot. I couldn't figgah out how fo' stand, so I jus stuck my hands in my pocket. Wuz getting mo' sweaty in there, but at least could wipe 'em off small kine.

I had my eye on Joy da whole night. I saw all da different guys she danced wit. I kept track of who she axed and who axed her. Not like I toll everybody I liked her ah, but cuz dey wuz invading my turf I had fo' put some of my friends on my doo doo list. I made da kine mental comparison fo' see wot all da guys she axed had in common fo' see if I had chance. Had chance. Every time one song came on I sed K dis goin' be da one, but every-time had one fass song and me I like take tings slow ah so I jus waited. I missed some opportunities wen da slow songs came on and befo' I could make my move some oddah girl came up to me. Befo' I could even make my move. Das my cool way of saying I nevah get any moves fo' make. But I wuz learning, making 'em up as I went along. I learned wea da bess place fo' stand wuz. Not by da wall cuz in case get one chic you like avoid. Need room fo' maneuver ah. Not by da punch bowl, cuz mo' chance you might spill on top you li'dat. Get all nerjous da hand start shakin' ah. Mo' worse you might spill on top her. In fack, James did dat and like da gentleman he wuz he offered fo' wipe 'em off her chess. Da stupid pervert. Da best place fo' stand wuz by all da Math Club peo-ple cuz you can look good ah. Hey I pretty smaht you know. Some girls I could ax. I wuzn't dat chicken, like some of my friends who made ME go ax fo' dem. "Oh, Carrie, James like you dance wit him. Nah c'mon, he really like you, you know. I promise he not going spill again. Aw c'mon. C'mon. C'mon. Pleeeeeeeeeease. Shoots, you going chance 'em den." See, easy fo' beg wen you not axing fo' your-self. See, I know all da secrets.

I no tink my Grandma would give her vote of approval for a lotta girls at dis dance. K, my Grandma would probably say dat Leslie is too fat. I mean, I not da kine superficial kine guy dat I only judge by looks. Wot I saying is dat da girl gotta be healthy looking. Eh, I like my potential wife live long time ah. And take Charisse. She too skinny my Grandma would say. I can dig dat. I like curves. I tink my Grandma would like hips cuz gotta have plenny grandkids ah. My Grandma would probably like breasts too cuz mo' healthy ah fo' my kid if he get breast milk. Da mo' plenny he get da mo' bettah ah. I no dig doze artificial kine formulas. Gotta tink all natural. Noting beats da real deals dude. Joy would be perfeck if wuzn't fo' dat ethnicity ting. I mean mo' bettah ah if she all mix up anykine. Cuz like dogs fo' example, those pure bred kine, dey die young. But da kine poi dog, dey live long time ah. Ho, conflict now dis kine rules.

Maybe wuz only to my eyes ah, cuz dey say beauty is in da eye of da beholder, but to me Joy wuz definitely a beauty to behold. Wuz almost twelve o'clock and wuz da lass dance of da night and had da Kool And The Gang song, "Cherish." Ho, of all da songs fo' pick, dat wuz my favorite song. Wuz kinda ol' already, but still I liked dat song. I could hear da sea gulls gulling. And my body started swaying side to side. I wuz all in la la land tinking of how perfeck would be jus me and her on da dance floor. Dis night would be da firs of many nights as tonight would be da night dat we would fall in love. As da chorus started playing I looked all ovah da room, looking, looking fo' Joy. She wuz gone. No tell me she went shi shi break. Not now. Wuz da lass song. No mo' songs aftah dis. No mo' songs tonight. No mo' songs evah. As I wuz getting all frantick, I started sweatin'. I could feel myself getting all hot. And wuzn't da kine good kine hot, but da kine nervous kine hot. Da kine hot dat dis going be one vital crossroads in my life kine hot. Da kine if I screw up tonight, den I going be one geek fo' da ress of my life kine hot. Ass why I wen go jump outta my Faddah's shoes wen somebody wen bump butts wit me from behind. Literally I wen jump ah cuz my Faddah's shoes wuz big. I nevah get dress shoes li'dat. I wen go bend down fo' fix my shoes and as I wuz tying da laces somebody wen go bang into me. Wen I looked up, staring right at me, wuz Joy. She sed "Oh excuse me." And wen I stood up again, she smiled and sed "Hi." I couldn't tink of anyting fo' say back, so I just sed "Hi." But wuzn't da kine simple kine "Hi," but one extended, gradually fading "Hiiiiiiiii" extending da "i's" hopefully long enough fo' me to add on someting at da end but unfortunately befo' I could come up wit anyting witty or clever to say, I ran out of breath.

I remembah my Grandma sed dat wen she and Grandpa got together she wuz only nineteen. At first Grandpa's dad nevah like her, but aftah a while he came to like her. Wen Grandpa's dad died Grandma wuz by his bed. She had fo' clean up his shi shi pan and stuff. He toll her tanks li'dat. She sed, "Remembah, befo' time you no like me remembah Otōsan?" He nodded weakly and sed, "Befo' time me no likey, but now me likey," and he put his hand on her hand. Da next day he jus nevah woke up. So I dunno why dey nevah like my Grandma. I tink someting about dey from different village back home or someting. I dunno, these ol'-fashion people not so smaht I tink. Cuz c'mon, you gotta figgah if you only can marry people in your village den pretty soon everybody going be all related and you going get all mutant kine babies.

My Grandma called me over to eat. She axed me wea my mom guys went. I toll her dey went PCT. My mom liked da monkeys. Usually my Grandma's food wuz pretty good, but today fo' some reason nevah get taste, but I nevah say noting. Fo' long time wuz quiet. Den she wen ax me one weird question. She sed, "Aftah you marry, wea you going buy house?" I toll her, "Uh, Kāhala Grandma. No worry I going fine one big mansion." Den she wuz silent. I dunno, my Grandma wuz acking all weird. She toll me dat wen I buy house, she no like me stay town-side cuz too much crime. She sed she no like me stay country-side cuz too abunai. So finally I toll her, "Den wea you like me live Grandma? No mo' no place else fo' go. Mainland? Ass worse." Den all of a sudden I wuz confuse wen she toll me SHE wanted fo' move. But she cannot move, I tot. Dis house get memories. Wen I wuz a leedle boy, every weekend I used to go my Grandma's house cuz she used to babysit me. Until I wuz like twelve around. Her house wuz always pretty cool cuz had da big mango tree outside. I used to love dat mango tree. My Grandpa used to pick 'em wit his stick ting and pass 'em down to my Grandma who wen stick 'em in one bucket. Every mango season we used to give all da neighbors. Sometimes people jus used to come by and ax for mangoes and my Grandma used to always give even if we nevah get dat much. Usually had plenny though. But da lass few years hardly had any and da few dat had people used to come and jus steal 'em li'dat. Had fo' pick 'em wen green cuz if we waited till wuz ripe would be gone. Lass year da tree had termite so dey wen chop 'em. Now she wanted fo' move. "Olaloa," she sed. She explained dat Olaloa stay Mililani side. Da suburbs? Olaloa supposed to be one gated community fo' old people or someting. There everybody look out fo' each oddah. More secure she sed. Mo' safe.

Wen Joy sed "Hi" to me wuz like major danger cuz dis wuz like new uncharted ground. Tings wuz easy wen me and Joy kept our distance. "Hi" from afar, never up close. Now we wuz talking in one social context. I cannot ax, "Oh, you wen do your homework?" "You wen study fo' da test or wot?" "Wot's da chemical symbol for Krypton?" Somehow, I knew we had a certain chemistry though. Could she possibly like me too? I mean, I not da most good looking guy in da world ah. Maybe by relative comparison to da dorky math guys around me, but definitely not da most good looking in da room. I mean, I not da smahtest, well maybe top ten percent. But maybe cuz I funny. Plenny people say I funny.

"Huh?" I sed as I realized dat she wuz talking to me and I wuz tinking too much to myself again. "I was asking you if you wanted to dance?" Wow, so wuz like she wuz saving dis last dance fo' me? Das so sweet yeah. I mean, who could turn down one line like dat? She wuz saving da lass dance fo' me. Meaning dat all da oddah guys she danced wit da whole evening befo' nevah really mattah. Michael Furoyama, Rommel Ofalsa, Ashley St. John, Kaha'i Logan, Kyung Taek Kang, Kyle Kurizaki, Brian Chong, Isaac Geiger, Tyrell Gospodarec, Kenneth Uedoi TWO TIMES, and Mr. Hirata all nevah mattah, cuz while she wuz dancing wit all dem, she wuz really only tinking about me. I dunno how long I took fo' answer but seemed like wuz, wuz, wuz one really long time. Dat whole night I dreamed of dancing wit Joy. But now I wuz having second tots. My hands wuz getting mo' sweaty now dat she wuz actually here. Pretty soon my pockets going get so wet going look like shi shi stain. Dis wuz like too fass fo' me. Me and her nevah even fass dance befo' and now I gotta make physical contact. Hands on hips? Hands

*34*

on da arch of her back? Or would we go allllllllll da way, hands completely around? I had no idea wea fo' put my hands wit her. Wot if I danced too close? Wot if my sweaty palms got her dress all wet? Wot if I stepped on her feet? Wot if I screwed up so bad dat everybody wuz going talk about me. Da entire sophomore class would probably gossip and make fun li'-dat and razz me fo' da rest of my high school career. Wuz I ready, wuz I prepared to take such a big risk? Finally aftah much contemplation I toll Joy, "Uh, I no feel like dancin'. . . . Uh, but you like talk? Maybe too noisy in here ah, uh . . . you like go outside talk story leedle while."

Outside wuz kinda quiet. Maybe too quiet. I jus leaned against da wall and formed a smile wit my lips as I looked at her. She apologized for banging into me. I explained wuz cuz da shoes. Den had plenny silent moments and I nevah know wot fo' say so I jus started bobbing my head and smiling wit my lips, hoping she would say someting. Soon. Da silence wuz broken wen all of a sudden, fo' no reason, she just started giggling. Mus be my shoes I tot? I toll my dad wuz too big fo' my feet and no need dress shoes cuz dis only wuz going be one cafeteria dance. I gave her my puzzled face and I axed why she wuz laughing. She sed she wuz tinking of da way I sed "hi" before. My "hi" sounded like a deflating balloon.

"Well das cause you knocked all da wind outta me," I sed.

"That's because I didn't see you."

"Why wuz you looking fo' me?"

"I almost didn't recognize you in your nice clothes."

"Why, you saying I usually dress all bummy?!"

"No, I like that aloha shirt."

"Ah ees okay. Wuz on sale. Did you see James' aloha shirt? His one is cool."

"Was it a blue shirt?"

"No, purple."

"Oh, I didn't look good."

"But . . . you always look good."

"Hah?"

"But you always LOOK GOOD."

And she looked puzzled fo' like two seconds befo' she finally caught on. Den she laughed so hard dat she made one piggy noise. Wit dat, she had me all laughing too and she covered her mouth and tings settled down fo' awhile, and den we jus started full-on laughing togethers. Finally, she calmed down and she offered me a compliment back, "And you're not so bad yourself."

"Why tanks, I've been saying my prayers and taking my vitamins."

"You mean, like Hulk Hogan?"

"How you knew dat? You watch wrestling?"

"Yeah, why? Is there someting wrong?"

"Oh no, you're weeeeeeeird."

And we jus talked and talked fo' hours. About wrestling. About how funny I wuz. About how weird she wuz. About if she could make any other animal noises wen she wuz laughing. About all kines of stuffs. We jus talked and talked aftah dat and befo' I knew it we talked fo' like almost an hour already. My Ma and Pa wen buss me wen I got home. My first time taking out da car by myself and I break curfew. Pretty stupid ah. But wuz worth. She gave me her number dat night and I called her da next day and we talked fo' almost da whole day.

I dunno how I could have so much fo' say den, but noting fo' say now. My Grandma wuz showing me her brochure for Olaloa and all of a sudden she jus started crying. I started fo' put my arm around her, but nevah feel like wuz da right ting fo' do. I mean she should be telling my mom dis, not me. Not my place fo' say anyting. But I

*36*

knew I needed fo' say someting so I sed, "No need go Olaloa Grandma. I come take care you." I dunno why I sed dat cuz not like I wuz ready fo' transfer school. What about Joy? And not like I can take care my Grandma. Not like I can cook. Not like I know how do laundry. I wen try one time and my fluorescent green T&C jacket came all Hypercolor. Not like I know how fo' do anyting. I jus got my license and I no tink I can take my Grandma anyplace, cuz town-side I dunno da roads so good.

Aftah a while, my Grandma calmed down leedle bit. She toll me dat Grandpa wuz moving to a nursing home. Ho, I wen look in fass kine wen I came in, but he looked da same. I jus assumed he wuz sleeping as usual. My Grandpa had hod time walking ever since his stroke. My Grandma sed dat fo' da pass couple weeks he wuz having problems eating so dey might have to feed him from one tube so he probably gotta go Maunalani nursing home up Wilhelmina Rise.

Wuz quiet fo' kinda long den she sed, "Tell your mom call me wen you get home, k." I nodded. She looked like she felt kinda awkward and I guess I did too. Cuz not like I evah saw my Grandma cry befo'. Only once wen I wuz shmall and she wen go give me spankings den I wen go pass by her room and I saw her crying on da bed. Now I felt like crying too, but Grandpa wuz kinda sick fo' long time already so we all kinda knew dat he wuzn't going get any bettah.

I jus sat there wit my hands closed together between my legs. Finally she sed, "You would come stay wit Grandma?" I nodded and she laughed. "You cannot take care Grandma. You still boy yet, you still going school." I wuz gonna argue dat I could transfer, but I knew she wuz right. She den changed da subject and axed me if I sent anyone a Valentine's. I toll her I jus sent out to one girl. She axed wot her name wuz. I toll her Joy. She den axed, "Wot her last name?" Den she gave me da lecture again. But midway thru she looked at me and stopped and she sed, "I guess nowdays cannot tell from lass name, no?" I nodded and she continued, "Maybe, no make difference. So long as you fine good kine girl, nahf. So long she take care you, Grandma happy." Den she axed me how my dance wuz. I toll her how long I talked to Joy on da phone. Approximate kine. Around eight hours. Forty-tree minutes. And twenny-two seconds. And I toll her how da firs ting I wuz going do wen I went home wuz check my mailbox. My Grandma sed, "No rush go drive wen you go home now." Den she sed, "Good you find girl. No fun wen you alone." Den it struck me. Wot if I wuz at da dance and no one axed me to dance. Wot if all da oddah guys in da Leo Club had da bubonic plague and I wuz da only guy in da room and Joy and all da oddah girls went lesbo and only danced wit each odder? Wot if no one cared for me den? Wot if no one cared for me ever? Wot a frightening tot it wuz fo' be all alone. I wanted to say something fo' stop my Grandma's watery eyes, but I came all teary-eyed too as I wrapped my arms around her, hands clasped tightly.

Wen I saw *Star Wars* wit my parents I wuz only five years old. Da line at Cinerama went all da way around da block li'dat. I tink I fell asleep toward da end, not cuz da movie wuz junk. But cuz I wuz so tired from waiting in da long line, out in da hot sun fo' like ova two hours. So good wuz, like one Disney movie, da kine you gotta take your kids go see one day. Too bad dey probably not going eva re-release 'em.

# distant galaxies

Joy and me wuz talking on da phone. I told her I found my Wicket. She liked da Ewoks so I wuz going give her mines. Not like wuz going break my set li'dat, cuz I had all da figures from da first two, but wen Jedi came out I wuz getting too old fo' toys li'dat, so I could part wit a few Ewoks.

Me and Joy wuz planning if we could go out dis weekend, but couldn't, cuz she sed she had to go to a family gathering and I toll her my grandma wuz making us go to one family gathering too. So hod fo' go out wit Joy. Evah since dat one time I came home late, my faddah wen crack down. "Driving da car is one privilege, boy. You lucky your faddah let you drive." Den he went off on his usual tangent on how he used to walk 5-10-15 miles to ol' Nagasako store. Everytime da store jus kept getting farther and farther away even though both his house and da store nevah move li'dat. And from there he usually went off sa'more on his recollections of how nowadays not like before kinda deals. And usually he jus kept talking on and on until you forget why he wuz talking in da first place and wot da point wuz and if there evah wuz one point. My faddah, he always going off on those tangents.

Now where I wuz? Today wuz Sunday and had football on TV so my faddah nevah like go to da 10-20-30 wotevah year memorial service. Plus, not like we Buddhist. My ma and pa guys part-time Christian, but my grandma wuz making everybody go. I knew da service wuz going be like one of those big family parties where all da aunties and uncles and cousins—first, second, third, calabash, anykine came and I had no clue who anybody wuz. Somehow all da aunties knew me though. Dey would go, "My Aaaaaaron, you're getting so biiiiig," and dey would slobber one kiss all ovah me and friggin' bear hug me li'dat. I hate wen dey do dat cuz not like I can retaliate ah. I betchoo half of dem no even remembah me. Only wen my mom goes, "Oh, you remember Aaron?" Of course dey going say yeah. Naturally I came big. I should hope so, da last time dey probably saw me wuz wen I wuz like fourt' grade. Naturally I going be taller ah. I should hope dat I wuzn't going be 4'2" fo' da rest of my life. Jus once I wanted say someting back wen dey went, "You coming big, yeah Aaron." Jus once I wanted fo' say, "Yeah auntie, and you coming big too." But I wuzn't da type to wise off. I jus tot dat in my head. Naturally, wen my ma axes me, "Oh you remember your auntie Deanna?" Of coss, I jus gotta

*40*

smile and nod my head even though I have no clue who she is. Like I wuz saying, not like I goin' know anybody. No point in me going. Nobody going miss me.

I only went to one funeral before and at least I met da guy ah. Wuz my dad's friend or someting. Scary ah wen somebody your age dies. If wuz one kid my age I tink I would be freakin'. Dis time wuz fo' one guy who wen ma-ke thirty-two years ago kine. So ass like way before I wuz even born. Uncle Lee is da guy. Dis guy no mo' da same last name as us. And not even same as my mom's maiden name. Somehow we wuz related though. Wot kine name is Lee? Maybe ees Haole. Could be black. Could be Korean too. I guess you jus don't know who you related to. At least I don't. So how's we related to dis guy? I guess somebody wen marry one Chinese maybe. Unless Lee is his first name. Eh, probably ah cuz why would he be Uncle Lee if Lee wuz his last name? So confusing.

Jus wen you tink you know, you don't know. Like in *Empire Strikes Back*. How wuz dat wen Luke found out dat Darth Vader wuz his faddah. Shocker yeah. I mean da galaxy so big, so wot's da odds dat Luke and Darth going get all reunited and battle. I remembah I saw 'em at da theater wit my faddah and wen da movie wuz pau I wen ax my dad, "Dad you really my dad yeah?" He got all mad. "Of coss boy, wea you tink you got all your handsome good looks, HAH?!"

My faddah is funny in dat he scoll my mom wen she drive slow li'dat. Today da service wuz someplace Kalihi-side and can tell he nevah like go wuz, cuz he wuz drivin' even mo' slow than my ma who's already one friggin' Sunday driver every day of da week. I wuz surprise cuz my ma wuz actually ready fo' go before him. Usually we all waiting insai da car while my faddah stay revving da engine, trowing da hint to ma dat TIME FO' GO ALREADY. Today we wuz going at like friggin' AT-AT speed, I guess cuz my faddah nevah know where he wuz going. My faddah missed da entrance cuz I guess he nevah went dis place before. I remembered coming here like lass year around. I went wit my grandma and grandpa guys. Before I met Joy, my grandma axed me go Bon Dance. Well actually, she nevah ask, more like she tricked me li'dat. She axed me, "Aaron, wot you doing Saturday?"

Usually she only ax fo' see wot I doing cuz she like know who I wuz hanging around wit. If I made any new Okinawan friends. And if I did, I knew da follow up question wuz going be, "Oh wot village they from?" Like anybody knows. We all go 'Aiea grandma, so we not from one village. 'Aiea is one city. We all from da city of 'Aiea. Das why we go 'Aiea High School. Anyway, I nevah like get into da whole village deals so I jus sed, "Oh, noting."

As you can see I wuz already trapped, cuz I sed I wuzn't doing anyting. I wuz committed.

"Good den. Go come wit me and grandpa."

"Where?"

"You go come Bon Dance. Fun you know."

Bull lie, fun. Junk Bon Dance. Da only ting good wuz da food. Tired walking round and round in one circle. Bull lie, my grandma sed get plenny nice kine girls. Well technically I guess I did meet some girls. Little girls like my cousin Mary-Ann's age. But not any my age li'dat. Had plenny nice ladies my grandma's age though.

42

We wuz sukoshi kine early fo' da memorial service. As we walked to da entrance of da jikoen, I noticed da circle outline painted on da ground. My ma explained to my pa dat wuz fo' wen dey get Bon Dance. He tot wuz fo' Dodge Ball or someting. I guess his parents nevah make him Bon Dance wen he wuz small. Da doors to da jikoen place looked so big. In da front had one stage wit golden pagoda-kine decorations. Had one shiny wooden podium on da side and da priest dude wuz doing stuffs. I wanted fo' cruise in da front row cuz had mo' leg room, but my ma wen kinda pull me toward da squishy cheap seats. My ma sed da close family supposed to sit in da front. I tink da closer you go da bettah you supposed to know da guy. In which case mo' bettah I go sit mo' back den, like way back, way back home li'dat, cuz not like I know dis guy.

And not like too comfortable too these wooden benches. Get one rack attached to da back of da benches in front of us. Reminds me of da airplane, but no' mo' noting fo' read. So I wonder hakum get these racks. Mus be fo' da *In Case of Emergency* pamphlets. In case Buddha fall from da sky, den dis is wot you do. I wonder hakum da movie theater seats get all cushions, but da church no mo'. If you like mo' people come, den jus make da seats mo' comfortable. Make sense, ah? Some refreshments would be good too. I try to tink if had one water fountain someplace. I cannot remembah.

Aftah a while da place fills up. Full house boy. Pretty big our family. I nevah knew I had so much relatives. Friggin' standing room only in da back. I guess get people even mo' distant than us. My grandma stay tearing small kine. Maybe I should give her some Kleenex. She bettah blow her nose now cuz da reverend guy stay coming up by da podium.

Aftah couple seconds da people quiet down and da reverend guy starts his speech. Everybody bows their head and so I copy.

"Na ha ma na na na ha ma na na na ha na o ko le le. Na ha ma na na na ha ma na na ahana kōkō lele." Well, not exactly, but someting li'dat. Eh, mento kine tings come to your head k, wen you're friggin' bored.

I guess he speaking clearly, but I cannot understand one word he saying. I trying fo' repeat but I jus end up making up anykine. He jus chanting someting in syllables. I remembah my ma axed me wen I wuz small if I wanted fo' go Japanese school. Wot fo'? I wuz tinking. Kikaida get subtitles. Why gotta learn Japanese? So wen my ma wen ax me, I jus sed, "Nah."

Getting sleepy already. Hakum he no talk English, dis guy? Half da people here mumbling 'em too, jus like me. Probably only people my grandma's age understand wot's da deals. My faddah he seems to pretty much know all da routine, but I no tink he knows da meaning ah.

Wen pau, everybody gotta go up in front and put sawdust in da big ashtray and bow their heads. Some guys put money. Big bills li'dat. My faddah busses out his wallet and gives my ma and me some money fo' go put too. I see and I do, but I no really know wot we doing. I hope dey no burn 'em. Cuz if dey going burn 'em den might as well give 'em to somebody who can use 'em, ah? Not like dey can use money in heaven ah. I dunno how their economy works up there, but I figgah money is evil cuz causes people to steal and stuff.

Aftah we do da whole money deals, I tinking "Okay pau. Time fo' go home watch foo-ball." But den da church guy starts talking. AGAIN. He asks everyone, "Do you know why we heah today? Most would say becauss of uncuru Ree. But does anyone know why else?" Den get one long pause before one guy finally yells, "Family?!" "Yahs becauzu ahf fa-mi-ly. We awru here to remem-

44

bah today uncuru Ree." He den starts talking about how we don't have to worry about uncle Lee cuz he's okay cruzing wit some pig guy, Amida Buta someting or another. He den talks about all da people in Japan who died in da Earthquake. Thousands died in their sleep during da quake. "Uncuru Ree's death reminds us thaht rife is freeting."

I'm tinking yeah life is "freeting." If life is fleeting den why don't you hurry it up so we can all bag li'dat. I raddah be going to Pearlridge wit Joy right now. I wonder wot she doing now? She probably having fun li'dat. I know she cannot wait fo' play wit my Wicket. Would be cool if me and her get married den someday we wouldn't have to worry about being separated cuz her family tings and my family tings would all be da same, cuz we would be part of da same family ah. I would have my own car. Porsche. Gotta go mother-in-law's house fass ah. So either one Porsche or one Ferrari. Joy can have one Honda or someting. Need someting fo' put da groceries in, ah? Den we would have like kids and we would make dem do fun stuffs. And we wouldn't force dem do stuffs dey nevah like do. Go places dey nevah like go if you get my driff.

I know you tink, ah, who's dis guy? He too young to be tinking of marriage yet. But you dunno me and Joy. We fated. Turns out dat both of us saw *Star Wars* on da same day at da same theater. Well I tink wuz only playing at dat theater—but at da same time too. She sed she went on da first day, first showing, jus like me. So someplace in da theater she wuz there. Wot's da odds? We wuz both in da same place, sharing in da same experience. Pretty cool, ah? She wuz there. I wuz there. We both wuz there. Fated I tell you. She sed she fell asleep too, but in da beginning cuz she wuz sked of Darth Vader so she closed her eyes fo' little while and she fell asleep. So between us we actually saw da whole ting. Me and Joy wuz tight. I knew everyting about her. EVERYTING. I knew her likes. Her dislikes. I knew she liked Penguin's Cookies and Creme. She liked Pepsi bettah than Coke. She didn't like dark chocolate, chocolate with almonds, chocolate with any kind of nuts. I knew she liked Popeye's chicken and she ate all da skin. I knew she liked her popcorn buttered wit extra salt. She put extra salt on her McDonald's fries. She put extra salt on her Stuart Anderson's prime rib before even tasting it. She even carried around little packets of salt— jus in case. Now das kinda unusual. I knew her—I knew her food.

All dis tinking about food. My stomach wuz grumbling while da priest-minister-pastor-reverend-dude-Bon-san, yeah das it, Bon-san dude wuz still talking. Aftah da service we went grine in da big auditorium room. Looking at all da guys I wouldn't guess dat we wuz all related. Even had one Pōpolo guy there. But I guess ees good dat get plenny ethnicities in our family, cuz maybe get mo' bettah kine food, ah? So we wen grab food li'dat and mingle little while. I knew I wuz going get da "Oh Aaron's getting so big." So I jus do da usual smile and nod. Finally, I give up asking my mom who wuz dat aftah each person leaves. Not like I going remembah anyway, ah, all da names. Everybody is either uncle or auntie or if dey young, den cousin. "Wassup Cuz." Simple ah?

Wuz it really necessary fo' me to go? Everytime aftah somebody left I would give my ma da "sigh . . ."—like c'mon we go bag already. She would jus give me da stink look like you bettah stop it now or else you going get one mean lecture wen we get home, young man. But I had one pretty good argument. I mean, if anybody ax where I stay, jus say, "Oh Aaron's going to college on da mainland already." Not like dey going know da difference. Everybody tink I big. Jus make me little bit mo' big. Say I going Med school at Yale in Colorado cuz I like be one Neuroscopomicrobatologist or someting dat sounds impressive.

So we wuz eating at da table and my parents and my grandma wuz talking to da minister guy. My grandma wuz asking him all kine Buddhist questions. I wuz all zoning. Playing wit my chopsticks wrapper. Bouncing 'em back and fourth between my hands. Back and forth. Back and forth I stay whacking 'em wen I jus accidentally whack 'em kinda hod and da ting goes flying and hits dis girl on da hand sitting way at da oddah end of da table. Aw, nah. Embarrassing now, I tinking, as I look away fas kine fo' make like wuzn't me. I look out of da corner of my eye trying fo 'see who I wen hit. She looked like she wuz one girl around my age. Kinda cute from far. Ho, das dirty. Wot I tinking? I in love wit Joy. And Joy's fully in love wit me. Why did I tink da girl wuz cute. Erase erase erase. Well, she might be ugly. Hod fo' see wuz cuz she wuz on da same side of da table as me. I no remembah my family guys talking to her and her family so dey must be real distant relatives I tot.

Suddenly I get startled wen my faddah looks at me and says, "Wot you doing, boy?"

"Noting dad."

"So hakum you get dat guilty face like you wen do someting? You nevah put noting inside my soda can, ah?"

"No."

"Why fo' you looking at dat girl?"

"Wot girl?"

"You met her before?"

"No, dad."

"Ass your . . . lemme see . . . well, if das da maddah, den her grandfaddah used to have da pig farm. Remembah we went their house wen you wuz small?"

So da grandfaddah mus be dat Amida Buta guy da reverend wuz talking about. I have no idea wot house my dad is talking about but I jus squinch my lips and nod.

"Come we go meet dem!"


Aw nah. So we wen stand up and walk ovah to dem. I tink my faddah jus wanted fo' get away from da Reverend guy cuz he wuz starting fo' play wit his soda can tab so kinda looked like he wuz bored like me. We went up to da lady and she and da girl wen stand up simultaneous. My faddah wen ax dem if their family still had da pig farm. I dunno why cuz not like he wuz trying fo' raise pig. But I guess kinda hod fo' start conversation ah, wit people you don't know. Not like you can tell da girl, who I cannot see now cuz da mom's robust figure stay kinda blocking da way, but so not like you can tell da girl, "Oh you getting so big, yeah?" I tink dat only works fo' guys li'dat.

Anyway, he introduces me to da mom, "You remembah auntie uh, Ber-nice, ah boy? We went their house wen you wuz one leedle keed, remembah?" I dunno how anybody expects me to remembah stuff from wen I wuz like only two years old. And not like my faddah get one good memory. So not like da good memory genes wuz passed down. My faddah, he cannot even remembah where he put da remote control half da time. In fack, him, he tink our house friggin' hi-tech, li'dat. Like we get voice activated remote control or someting wen he say, "Aaron go change 'em Channel 2" and I gotta go stand up and go change 'em. And usually wen I change 'em I stand up there

*48*

little while, cuz I know as soon as I go sit back down he going say, "Aaron, go change 'em back Channel 4." We need one new TV, man.

So anyway, I jus smile and make like I remembah wot their pig house wuz like. Probably wuz stink. Kinda like auntie Bernice's perfume. I dunno why, but these old aunties dey jus take one bath in perfume must be, cuz so potent wen dey come in fo' da hug. My face stay all half grimacing, partly from da perfume, but partly cuz I know wot's coming next. Ees like my face is da Deathstar and her mouth is one whole fleet of X-Wing Fighters flying in fo' bombard me wit kissing missiles. "Aaron you're so cuuuuuuute." Kiss kiss kiss kiss kiss kiss. Stop already. Save some fo' some oddah stranger boy. I surprised dat my face nevah get all sucked up yet. My face probably going be all deformed now wen I go home. I going look like friggin' Darth Vader witout his mask on and Joy will nevah love me da same again.

Or would she? Cuz me and Joy get someting special, ah? I mean maybe me and her bettah go have one talk, but I dunno, wot if I get like all hair on my chess like my faddah and I come like friggin' Chewbacca? Den would she still love me? Wot if her body got all had-it and she started looking like Jabba da Hutt, would I still love her? Me and Joy had like one special kinda love, I tink. Da only ting dat maybe might keep us apart is death. A love dat transcends all obstacles. I tink my love fo' Joy is pretty much eternal, ah? Junior Prom, den Senior Prom, den we'll get engaged, den aftah college we'll get married. If she died tomorrow, I dunno wot I'd do. I mean cuz our whole life is pretty much mapped out already, ah? It's like written in da stars.

I squint my eyes couple times as auntie Uh-Bernice steps to da side fo' introduce her daughter. I close my eyes and open dem again, hoping I nevah saw wot I saw. My faddah goes, "Oh, I almost nevah see you dea. Aaron, dis your cousin. Ho she really grown up since da last time I saw her. Aaron, you remember uh, uh Jane ah. No no no. Uh, uh, uh."

"JOY!?" I yell.

And all surprised my faddah goes "Yeah Joy, ho, you get good memory, ah boy? I must've passed down all my smaht genes to you li'dat."

*Return of The Jedi*. To me Han wuz cool, but Luke would've made one bettah husband. Wot kine values Han going teach his kids? You saw how he wen snuff Greedo, ah? Rootless. He one drifter. He probably get one chic in every spaceport. Did Luke evah kiss Leia or wot? I know Leia kissed Luke on da cheek. Did dey kiss on da lips? If dey did, den das kinda gross. Dey kinda avoided da conflict between Luke and Han. I wondah hakum—dey not Asian. George wen cut dat scene I tink. I guess cuz dey wanted da feel good ending. But I wonder how Luke really felt.

I nevah got around to giving Joy my Wicket. In school Joy wuz still friendly to me. But we nevah kissed in da back of my faddah's Monte Carlo, in back of R building, in da grassy hill by Nahele Park, we nevah kissed anywhere again. I felt like questioning. I mean not like we wuz first cousins. I don't even tink we wuz second or third cousins. We had so much fo' say, but we jus didn't. We went back to da friendly Five Finger Linger Waves. An occasional call jus fo' see wot's new. I rehearsed in da mirror fo' days wot Luke might've sed: "Sorry Princess, our ancestors wuz from da same village on Planet

Alderaan, Alderon—how you pronounce 'em? I don't want no mutant babies, so you bettah forget about me. Go on wit your life." Friggin' Yoda's parents wuz probably related li'dat.

And wit Obi Wan and Yoda gone, who going be leff fo' pass on da ways of da Jedi—da ways of da Force? Only get Luke, only Luke leff, cuz Leia don't know noting. Somehow, though, dey bettah pass on all their ancient Jedi secrets oddah wise going be loss fo' da future generations. If Luke and Leia did do da deed, dey would probably, wit their powers combined, would have one real kick ass Jedi kid, friggin' ugly as hell, but a real powerhouse. I guess Luke nevah practiced wot he wuz going say. He nevah really tot of breaking up Han and Leia and trying fo' get back in wit her. Cuz he probably nevah tot someting li'dat would evah happen. You would tink wot's da odds in one galaxy so big. Wot about on one island so small?

*Trick-O-Treat. Trick-O-Treat. Gimme someting good to eat.* Wuz jus li'l aftah six wen we heard 'em. "Wo wo wo wo. Dey stay coming already," I could jus hea my faddah tinking as his eyes blossomed wide open. "We not even

# black leather hot

pau eating and den. Da sun nevah even go down yet. I still watching da news li'-dat. Parents should at least make 'em stay home and watch da weather first, you no tink so? Serve dem right if rain. Kids nowadays," my faddah shook his head and mumbled undah his breath while he stood up to go look fo' some scratch papah.

Dis year my faddah wuz trying fo' pass da buck and he wanted ME fo' stay home pass out candy. I toll 'em, "Cannot cuz Robin going come get me pretty soon. Go make ma do 'em." Nobody wanted fo' do 'em dis year. Before, my ma used to like pass out candy. Used to get plenny cute little kids. Now she refuses. She sez, "The neighborhood has grown up. Only high school kids come to our house now. They come roller blading around with their extra-large pillow cases to hold all their candy. And they're too lazy to even wear a costume, I tell you. And when I confront them on the fact that they're not dressed up, they have the nerve to answer back and say that they ARE dressed up, dressed up as students. That's not dressing up." In one last attempt fo' try and get out of passing out da candy my faddah wrote someting on one piece papah and suggested dat we go stick da candy in one basket and leave 'em on da porch and jus put one sign dat says "Please take ONE." Like dat going work I tot. Probably all going be gone aftah da first group of kids come.

I tot my faddah wuz serious about his sign ting, cuz he wuz taping someting to da door as we heard da kids running down Mr. Cabral's driveway. Cracked me up wen I saw wot he wrote: "We open promptly at 6:30." He tot dat dat would teach da rude kids one lesson and so next year dey wouldn't come so early. I tink he figured dat da kids who came early would jus pass our house and move on, but wuz funny cuz wen he opened da door at 6:37 had one long line of kids all waiting. I guess cuz da first couple kids figured dat, "Ooh dis house muss have good candy if we gotta wait." And den da kids dat came aftah dat saw da line starting to form so dey must've figured dat, "Ooh get one line li'dat. Muss have someting gooood at dis house." Typical crowd mentality. Kids is always monkey see, monkey do ah.

Yesterday, I toll my dad, "Buy chocolate kine now, bumbye somebody going egg our house you know, cuz you so chang." He sed, "Sucking kine mo' bettah cuz lass mo' long. Da kids going appreciate cuz . . ." And befo' he could start his "Back in my days story" I jus sed, "Yeah, yeah, yeah, I undahstand," cuz I nevah like hea da story again ah about how he nevah have candy wen he wuz small and how wuz one TREAT fo' eat da orange peel wit sugar on top. Da orange PEEL you know. Not da actual orange, but da orange PEEL. Strong emphasis on PEEL cuz dey wuz POOR.

Even though I wuz standing behind, I could jus see my faddah wit da egg on his face. Cuz I saw all da li'l kids' sour puss looks as he gave 'em all only one-one ah, while dey probably all wuz tinking to themselves, "You mean . . . WE . . . waited in line . . . jus . . . fo' ONE . . . friggin' . . . Jawbreaker?" Yuuuup. Tot you wuz going get something good ah, well now you can—wop your jaws.

"Don't forget Aaron, you have school tomorrow. You better make sure you're back at the dorms early now," my ma yelled as I wuz about to leave da house. She axed me wea I wuz going. I toll her Robin wuz going come get me den we wuz going Rob's house. Actually us tree wuz going cruise Waiks den go Restaurant Row, but I nevah like her worry ah. She hates it wen we go Waiks cuz I guess get all kine crime ah. I tink das mostly da tourist people getting hijack. But my ma says dat Waikīkī is da crime capital of da state. She always watches da news about all da drive-by shootings and stuff. But not like I wen lie to her wen I sed I wuz going visit Rob, cuz Robin wuz going pick me up, den we wuz going Rob's house, fo' pick up Rob. I just nevah toll her da full agenda. Jus as I wuz stepping out, my ma reminded me, "Don't forget your jacket." Dat gave me one idea fo' one bettah costume. I wuz planning to go Rob's house and borrow his old Dracula costume, but stale ah. So I wen go back grab my faddah's old black leather jacket from da closet. We wuz hoping some of da girls would wanna come out wit us, but frick tonight I tink we jus had fo' tattoo da big "L" on our foreheads cuz we were Losers. We wuz hoping Jamie would come cuz she wuz a honey, but she sed her church no believe in Halloween. Halloween is Satan's night or someting. If you go Trick-O-Treat den you worshipping Satan. I tried fo' convince her dat ees jus one commercial celebration ah. Like how much people who celebrate Christmas actually worship Christ and God li'dat. Anyway, she sed she wuz going stay home and read her Bible. So we wen down our list and Michelle guys had fo' study. Jenny and Cari had some sorority party ting dat I guess we wuzn't invited to. Lisa, Lori had one party their place, but we nevah like go cuz only going get da same gang and dey only play friggin' Taboo and Pictionary all night long. We wanted fo' meet some women in our lives and hopefully find dat evah elusive love of a lifetime.

Halloween used to be one big ting in Hawai'i. I remembah da time I wuz six and wuz raining supah hod on Halloween night, so Governor Ariyoshi wen postpone 'em fo' make all da kids happy. Dat wuz cool. If he wuz running today, I'd vote fo' him. Nowdays, da candidates all junk; dey only talk stink about each oddah. My faddah sed dat wen I wuz small, my muddah used to make Hawaiian Punch and chocolate chip cookies li'-dat, give all da kids. Nowdays, if you do dat people probably going tink you friggin' nuts. Dey going tink you put nails in da cookies and rat poison in da punch. Nowdays, you hardly see any big groups li'-dat, walking around da neighborhood. I hear dat some neighborhoods dis year no mo' even Halloween. Dey jus get da kine candy exchange at da school cuz da church groups no like da kids walking da streets at night cuz of da recent gang murders. I no remembah we had stuff li'dat before. Everybody my school used to Trick-O-Treat. We all grew up same neighborhood ah—Stephen Rice, Shannon Maialoha, Shannon Shigehara, Jeff Nugent, Jackie

Chun, Tino Gonsalves, Rommel Ofalsa, Sunu guys. Ho, we had choke guys in our group. And we nevah like girls tag along, but you know da kine ah, everybody get their sistah or cousin or someting and so den dey all gotta come along too ah, but wuz okay cuz we nevah discriminate.

But I can see why kids hardly go nowdays. Mostly da parents take 'em March of Dimes Haunted House. Before, everybody used to pass out candy; now only get like houses here and there kine. Not worth. Da street mostly dahk Halloween. I tink people purposely turn off their light so dey can friggin' hide out and watch TV in da dahk so nobody go their house. We used to spend da whole night till ten, cuz da mo' long we go, da mo' candy we get ah. Nowdays kids, dey only Trick-O-Treat fo' like one hour li'dat. No mo' stamina kids nowdays I tell you boy. Eh, I starting fo' sound like my faddah already. And da kids, dey lucky cuz da parents chauffeur 'em around house to house. I guess dey need one car, cuz dem, dey all like go up Cadillac Hill, Summit side cuz das where all da rich guys pass out good chocolate kine, Snickers, Peanut Butter Cup li'-dat. Before time we nevah used to target specific areas. And we nevah used to go around in cars, we used to walk, wit our feet. Ho, I really starting fo' talk like my faddah now. I dunno how else you going walk yeah, wit your hands, I don't tink so. And nowdays kids junk. I bet dey proud dey get one, two bags. Me, I always used to bring home like five grocery bags. Dis wuz my secret—I always tried fo' be da first guy in line ah so den I could run to da back and put on one noddah mask so I could get candy again. Smaht ah me. Wah wah, nahting wrong. Only innocent fun li'dat. Innocent fun.

56

*Trick-O-Treat. Trick-O-Treat. Gimme someting*
*good to eat. If you don't, I don't care.*
*I'll pull down your underwear.*

HONK. HONK. Ho das Robin. He nevah need honk. Could hear da rumbling from his Z28 coming from down da street. One of da most awesome muscle cars on da island. Not as cool as Uncle Alvin's El Camino, but it definitely blew da doors off Norm's Baracuda. Well maybe das cuz Norm still nevah pau put da engine insai, but even if he did he still couldn't touch Robin's Camaro.

Dis year Robin wuz Sir Lancelot. He even had da full on knight kine helmet, everyting. Surprise me, cuz usually he no spend money on his costume. I tink he wen borrow 'em from da theater department. Last year he wen put grease on his face and he brought one screwdriver. I sed, "Wot you supposed to be—mechanic?" "No, car thief," he sed jokingly.

Wen we got to Rob's house we wuz all laughing wen he came outside wearing his Aunty Shige's "natural" blonde wig and his faddah's old bathrobe wit shiny kalakoa sequins jus stuck on top anykine. "Wot you supposed to be, one flasher?" I axed. "I am da Nature Boy, Ric Flair. Woo!" Rob proudly annouced. As for me, I had my costume going too. I used Robin's comb fo' slick my hair. I rested my shades on top my head. I splashed on some Cool Water cologne, so I guess you could say I immersed myself in cool. And fo' da finishing touch, I donned my black leather jacket. Yup, tonight I wuz goin' be . . . da Fonz.

We wen park by da Waikīkī Theaters and Robin leff his helmet in da car. Bumbye da girls cannot see his handsome face ah. Aftah walking around Waiks fo' like an hour we wuz tired of seeing like fifty guys dressed up like dicks.

Wuz funny last year wen we saw one guy do 'em, but da effeck is loss wen everybody copy ah. I dunno if those guys dumb or jus plain dumb. Like you going impress one chic wit one penis costume. I don't tink so. Anyway, da only cute chic we saw wuz dis chic who looked like Brooke Shields. She wuz accompanied by dis guy who wuz dressed like Michael Jackson. He looked pretty much like da King of Pop, only he wuz like ten times mo' tick. Rob started staring too much at Brooke, so before Michael came ovah fo' broke our asses, we headed fo' da Row where all da action usually wuz.

Ho, da place wuz packed. Plenny Batmans, vampires, witches, and baseball players. Aftah scoping da scene, we decide fo' go check out Blue Zebra. And aftah waiting till Christmas in da long ass line we finally got in. I wanted fo' pull down my shades so I could check out da babes. I see you. But you don't see me. Incognito ah. But kinda weird ah you wear shades indoors and plus nighttime ah. Insai, had one cute girl dressed like Chun Li from Street Fighter, but she wuz already attached to dis guy who looked like Guile wit his army fatigues and hair all spiked vertical wit Ice Mist. Wot's wit these couples?

Da house wuz rockin' and dey already had some kinda dance contest going on. Luckily we saw some girls we knew. Heather, Kathy guys wuz there. Good, back up ah. "Whoomp There It Is" wuz cranking on da speakers. We sed "Hi" to some oddah girls we knew, but we wuzn't sure if dey saw or heard us, yeah. Da place wuz mo' full than Akebono's stomach at one all you can eat buffet. We barely had time fo' soak up da atmosphere wen suddenly we heard all da guys whistling and shouting "Whoooooyaahh!!!!" We looked to wea everyone's attention wuz focused.

58

Every guy had his eyes on dis one hot-awesome babe. If she wuz a potato, she'd definitely be a hot potato, I tell you boy. She wuz one Local girl wearing tight black leather shorts wit imitation snakeskin accents and one leather cowboy type vest. She look li'l bit older than us and we nevah know who she wuz supposed to be dressed up as, but we liked her. Definitely a deucer. I don't really know wot her most attractive feature wuz cuz I had all of two seconds fo' study her wen she suddenly started taking off her vest and danced around in jus her bra. And ho, she wuz definitely getting more jiggle for her wiggle, more bounce per ounce there. I dunno if dems wuz da real deals, but we nevah care. She wuz right there live and in person practically bouncing her beautiful breastesses in our faces. Everybody's drool wuz jus practically falling into her cleavage I tell you. Usually you gotta go Ke'eaumoku fo' get one show dis good, oh oh, I mean so dat I heard ah. Cuz you would tink dat someting like dis would nevah happen here. Restaurant Row supposed to be pretty much uptown ah. Ho, some guys on da oddah side wuz holding out their dollar bills li'dat. I wuz waiting fo' da security guard go tell her haul her act down Hotel Street or someting. But I guess da bouncers wuz enjoying da nice surprise too ah. Us guys all tot she wuz going win da dance contest, but da judges gave da prize to some oddah chic. Heather wuz all like, "Good for her, the slut." Aftah tings settled down, we wuz getting pretty tired dancing wit jus Heather guys. Of coss, you all know who we wanted fo' dance wit.

We huddled together. Okay keiki. Dis is it. Da championship game. "Wot's da deal, lemon peel?" I axed. We wuz trying fo' figure out our plan of attack—who should go first. Robin wuz all quiet, while me and Rob wuz getting all hyped, getting into da zone. Finally, Robin decreed dat he wanted fo' go last. I suppose he wuz probably tinking dat me and Rob wuz going strike out so would be up to him ah, he gotta step up and save da day. Him, he always gotta be da show-off, big-stud hero ah. Just once I wanted fo' show him.

Rob went first. "Watch and learn, you poseurs." Wenevah we went clubbing we always used to call Rob "Da Slyder" cuz he wuz always on da sly wen he wen try fo' slide in fo' make 'em to home base. Dis slide in approach wuz da tried and true method wea you jus start dancing and slowly you get closer and closer to da girl you like dance wit. Dirty ah. I hate wen guys do dat. Well, I suppose dat sliding might have worked if Rob had room to slide. Seems like every oddah guy in da place wen go shnake Rob's patented technique. All dejeck-ed, Rob came back and toll me wuz my turn fo' chance 'em next.

I figgah mo' bettah wait fo' da break and den make my move. I figgahed dat maybe if I talked to her we could form some kinda connection ah and move beyond jus da physical attraction. Actually, she wuzn't really my type. Kinda too slutty fo' me, but I guess part of me jus wanted fo' take da title of Stud King away from Robin ah. Ho, wuz going be even mo' hod fo' me, cuz she wuz now cruising wit her girlfriends li'dat, so wuz going be hod fo' try steal her away. I hate wen dey stay in packs li-dat. May-jah dayn-jah ah, cuz always get chance dey going do da bait and switch. Must avoid da bait and switch.

I gathered my courage and jus as I wuz about to go in these two military guys wen go rush 'em. So I had fo' make real casual as I made da pivot and walked back to da boyz. I had my back turned to her while Rob and Robin gave me da play by play on wot wuz going down. She turned both of dem down. Losers! So once again I got

*60*

psyched. Rob wuz all like, "Goin' bu, goin', you da man!" So I styled and profiled over in her direction one mo' time, but dis tall GQ wannabe guy in one faggy looking International Male swashbuckler shirt cut me off and he beat me to da punch. I kinda made my way pass da Stripper Chic to over by Heather guys fo' make like das wea I wuz going all along. I overheard part of their conversation. She sed, "No tank you, I resting. Maybe later." Das girl talk fo' "Scram you ham!" So I decided NOT fo' get psyched up any mo' and jus go. No style, no technique, jus go psycho. So I quickly strided over to her and sed, "Ayyyyye, I'm Aaron, but you can call me uh . . . Aaron." I gave her da cool tumbs up and jus sed da first ting dat came to mind, "Uh, cool costume." Yup, real smooth. I den tried to establish rapport as I axed her, "Wot's your name?" She sed her name wuz Jennifer. I decided to jus be upfront and ax her to dance. I mean she already had one good five minutes fo' rest ah. Das plenny time. So I axed her. She said "No, das okay." Ho da hurtin'. Insai I wanted fo' plead and grovel, but I sed, "Yeah, maybe next time den ah," and I slinked back to da corner wea da boyz wuz having a good chuckle. Gee, I wuzn't even good enough to make up one excuse fo'. At least she toll da oddah guy dat she wuz resting. "So wot bu, wot happened?" Rob axed faking his concern. I got her name I announced proudly. Dey den inquired if I got any oddah valuable information, like her phone number. Posturing back my shoulders I sed defiantly, "Of coss, of coss I got her phone number." Dey den axed dat I produce da evidence. Even if I did get 'em, like I would share 'em wit dem ah. Anyway, I cracked, and aftah much physical interrogation, I coughed up da fack dat I got nowhere wit her.

It looked extremely gloomy fo' all da guys who wuz there dat day. Da score wuz 0 fo' 5 wit jus one guy leff fo' play. Cuz now Robin, mighty Robin wuz advancing to da bat. So we drew da big "S" on his chest and wished him luck. We studlings knew he wouldn't fail us. Girls always dig him ah. Like one Calvin Klein bibadee model, Robin cruised confidently over to wea da Stripper Chic wuz standing. To our surprise, he returned aftah talking wit her fo' like less than a minute. He came back to our corner . . . ALONE?! Mighty Robin had struck out. He sed dat she toll him dat she only digs hapa kine guys. Hakum seems like all da girls nowdays like hapa kine guys? Wow, dat wuz low. I tink I liked my short and sweet "No" bettah than dat. I mean Robin cannot help da fact dat he not hapa. Robin must've been all traumatize, cuz normally I could jus imagine him coming up wit one good comeback, someting like: "But I am, hapa. I'm only half mortal."

Ho, Robin must've been in shock. He takes great pride in his appearance. He proud dat he's Mr. Everyting a woman could evah want in a man. Jus a "Total Package" Lex Luger I tell you. He get one cool Camaro, he sings and plays da 'ukulele good, he smart, well maybe he jus ack smaht, but I guess he's of above average intelligence, he get one direction in life—business major ah, he get membership at Gold's and he uses 'em, plus he spends hours on his hair. To fault him fo' da fack dat he not of mixed ancestry is jus cruel and unusual punishment. I mean das like da one ting he cannot help. No girl evah rejeck-ed him cuz of his ethnicity. Das friggin' prejudice. Wot kine world we live yeah? Suddenly, despite all her exterior beauty she became da ugliest girl we've evah laid eyes on. And believe me now wen I tell you later, us guys have laid our eyes on many a girls.

*62*

Ho, Robin wuz pissed. He jus walked out li'dat. So natural we followed him ah cuz we wuz concern fo' our ride, um, I mean, concern fo' our friend bu, concern fo' our friend. Plus Heather and Kathy guys wuz all dirty dancing so I no tink we could count on dem fo' one ride. Dat reminds me I bettah go tell Kathy's bruddah wot his underage sistah wuz doing wit dat horn dog over there. She shouldn't be doing da kine stuff she wuz doing. Anyway, da whole night wuz pretty much ruin. Da whole drive Robin wuz all swearing, "Fuck her, man! What's her problem, fuck. Fuck the bitch. She thinks she's so bad. She's just a frickin' flirt. A teaser. Just a fuckin' tease, man. She was right there in our faces. In our faces man, and she just treats us like dirt. If we never had a chance, then why the hell did she friggin' do all that wiggle and jiggle crap right in front of us then?!"

Fo' long time wuz quiet. Da tension wuz all heated wen Robin sed intensely, "What can I do, God made me the way I am, right?" We agreed in a unified response. Den he became real serious as he posed to us dis question: He sed, "If nobody would ever find out, and if there wasn't a God, would you guys ever force yourselves on a hot-awesome babe like the Snake Skin Stripper Chic?"

But I sed, "Isn't God always watching?"

"Hypothetical hypothetical, and she'll have no memory of it either so she'll never testify against you or anything," Robin added.

"Oh, so you mean use dat illegal date rape drug like dey get now," Rob sed.

"Whatever Rob, just answer the question."

"I dunno. Maybe, but not as fun wen da girl not into it, ah?"

"Yes or no?" Robin sed kinda loud—half joking, half not. I laughed a little and made like I wuz still pondering Robin's question cuz I still nevah have one answer. Wenevah Robin axes a question, ees usually jus cuz he get someting dat he like say. So finally he sed dat he would still do da slut. To teach her a lesson he sed. "So what about you Aaron, would you TREAT yourself to her," Robin laughed at his own pun. Robin lifted his chin signaling dat he wuz still waiting fo' my answer. I jus made one popping sound wit my lips. I tot about da girl Jennifer in her leather outfit. I tot about all da Halloween costumes at da dance. I tot about all our Halloweens wen we wuz small, my friends from da old neighborhood, da candy we used to get, da fun we used to have, da *Trick-O-Treat, Trick-O-Treat* song we used to sing.

And as da warm night air chorused into da car Robin axed me again wot I would do. "Well? Well?" Robin repeated. Wuz only couple seconds, but seemed like wuz long time wen finally I tilted my head and I answered "No" and jus leff it at dat. I took off my Fonzie jacket cuz wuzn't cool anymore and I lowered down my shades and stared through da windshield as we drove off into da dahk.

My parents nevah raised no dummy ah. Wuz my second semester at UH and I desperately wanted some transportation. At least one moped so I nevah need walk to class and plus wen da boys go shoot pool or someting I no like dey always pack me ah. Freedom. Independence li'dat. In order fo' convince my faddah, I knew dat I couldn't jus ax him straightforward, "Oh pa, can get one moped?" Cuz I knew he jus goin' say "No!" and dat goin' be da end of dat conversation. Most oddah of my friends would probably use da argument, "Oh, but Warren and Paul get one." But I know dat not going work fo' my faddah. He mo' smaht than dat. He probably jus going say, "Too bad you not Warren or Paul den yeah."

So hod fo' win wit my faddah. I remember high school time I wanted fo' supe up his car and make 'em mo' stylin' li'dat. Cuz hod fo' be cool, wen da car only get da kine AM radio ah, if you know wot I mean. I wanted fo' get one Alpine deck wit Bazooka bass, but my faddah lowered da boom on dat plan, wit yet another one of his clever ways of saying "No!"

"So wot dad, can get sounds or wot?"

"Aaron, we cannot get stereo. No mo' alarm."

# wheeling and double dealing

"Oh yeah, yeah. We go put theff deterrent den."

"Theff deterrent? Wot fo? No mo' noting fo' steal."

My faddah's one sneaky buggah ah. Das why I wuz tinking, you know wen you selling one used car, you not goin' put da exact amount dat you really like get. Of coss you goin ax fo' way mo' than wot you expecting. Dat way you get room fo' bargain down ah. Das why wen my mom and dad wuz at da dinner table, I wen look at my mom and say real casual, "Ma, I like one motorcycle." Naturally she wen freak. She wen rant on about, "Don't you know Aaron how dangerous it is to ride a motorcycle blah blah blah."

"No worry ma, I goin' wear one helmet," I sed. And plus I toll her dat my friend Darin wuz already teaching me. She wen turn to my faddah to talk some sense into me. He sed, "Boy, wot fo' you need motorcycle?!"

I toll him about how hod wuz fo' make 'em to class, "Far y'know dad, gotta walk from Bus-Ad to Moore in fifteen minutes."

Das wen my faddah wen zone out and go into one of his stories about da old hanabata days. "Back in my days boy, wen me and my bruddah, yo' uncle, yo' uncle Alvin, wuz goin' UH we nevah get motorcycle you know, nevah even get roads back den. We nevah get da kine fancy kine auditoriums like how you guys get now. In fack, you know wea da Varsity Theater stay, we used to walk all da way dea fo' lecture classes. Walk, you know. Wit our feet! See boy, you lucky."

He tot he had me on da ropes wit dat one, but I wuz prepared, I knew he wuz gonna go in fo' da knockout blow.

"Plus boy, how you goin' get da money fo' buy one motorcycle, HAH?! You know you gotta pay insurance you know. Tell me wea you goin' get dat kine money?"

"I get 'em all figured out pa, Darin goin' sell me his old Kawasaki Ninja, cuz he like buy one Yamaha FZR. So he goin' give 'em to me cheap. I get enough saved up from my summah job. So wot dad, can?"

My mom's timing couldn't have been more perfect wen she interrupted, "Daddy, motorcycles are too dangerous. You cannot let Aaron ride. You remember in the paper, the boy who was riding in Mililani whose head got decapitated by the big trailer?"

Das wen I knew I had dem. I know dey nevah like ME be one noddah accident statistic, so I sed, "I promise I not goin' drive fast . . . please dad."

Finally aftah couple of "Please dads" my faddah sed, "K, boy dis da deal den, since you already get da money. Remembah now, ma and I not goin' help you pay noting. Motorcycle too dangerous fo' you. No son of mine is evah riding one motorcycle. I dunno why dey make 'em can go 150 mile per hour, wen da speed limit only 55. I know you cannot handle dat much power. But, since your faddah is one nice guy, he goin' make you dis deal. If you want, you can buy . . . one moped. Dat way you cannot go mo' fast than wot, 30 mile per hour. But I no like you go around gala-vanting all ovah da place now. So jus remembah, if your school grades drop den you going back to foot mobile, k? So wot son, deal?"

"But daaaad," I whined, but inside I wuz all like, "Chiiii! Damn I'm good."

I got one used Yamaha Razz from my friend Cary's store on Kapahulu, Moped Masters. He gave me one good deal, plus he always went Japan li'dat so he threw in some parts for supe 'em up. Could go like 50 now which wuz pretty cool. His one wuz super nice. Had spoiler on top and he made 'em so could go friggin' 70. Das too fas for me. Anyway, I knew now dat wit dis great power I now had a great responsibility. I had a responsibility to chauffeur all da hot-awesome babes from lower campus to upper campus. I knew my R-A-Z-Z wuzn't no FZR, but hey my friend Toby used to pack girls on his moped all da time. Just gotta make like "Oh, do you need a ride" and BUYA she's in back holding onto you like friggin' gum stuck on top your rubbah slippah.

Dat wuz how I met my girlfriend, Marlene. Marlene wuz one cute girl from Maui, '88 Baldwin grad. She had sad squinty kine eyes, but she wuz always smiling. She dressed pretty neat, cuz business major ah. And she wuz pretty solid. I knew my faddah would approve of her, not only cuz she wuz pretty, but cuz she wuz from Maui. Da first day wen I moved into da dorms he said, "Boy, wen you find girlfriend, make sure she from da neighbor islands." "Why?" I asked. "Cuz you know she not goin' go home on da weekends, and she not goin' have friends fo' go out wit, so she can do your laundry on Saturday-Sunday." Den he laughed as my muddah wen go slap his arm "Daddy!"

Marlene lived Lokelani, same floor as my good friends Rob and Robin, so I always used to cruise ovah there. Dem guys always had their doors open so Marlene and her friends would always trickle in. Marlene had one pink moped, but it broke halfway through da semester and she nevah have enough to pay fo' da repairs. Me, being da gentleman dat I wuz, offered to give her a lift to Bus-Ad cuz we had class at da same time. I knew she wuzn't going say no, cuz her accounting class wuz all da way at da oddah end of campus. Since she wuz already moped dependent I knew she wouldn't refuse.

My friend Rob wuz from Hilo. He wuz one wrestler dude wit short spiky hair and he played da trumpet in da band. Weird combination yeah, geek-jock. Dey used to call him "Da Python" cuz that wuz his finishing maneuver. He used to play possum den spring his python move and make da oddah guy submit by squishing his body wit his tick ass legs.

Robin wuz one tall Chinese guy from Leilehua. During his breaks he would always come back to da room to fix his hair. He had da sides fully gelled and he always used to spray and blow dry da front fo' make sure his wave had da full visor-like extension going on. And den, he would look in da mirror, and make like da kine Andy Bumatai ah, "Ehhh you handsome buggah, you still get 'em." Robin wuz pretty much da stud of our group. He had some of da corniest bullshit lines for pick up girls. Like, he would say, "Oh do you have a map?" Den she would say, "Oh no, why?" "Cuz I get lost in your eyes." Dumb ah. Half da time I tink dey not even listening to wot he wuz saying, but he such one stud dat he could probably say any stupid dumb ass ting and dey would go all goo-goo gaa-gaa.

Both Rob and Robin played da 'ukulele fo' fun and das why da girls always came ovah to their place fo' sing and cruise li'dat. Me, I could sing okay, but sometimes I wish my maddah and faddah had da foresight fo' send me Roy Sakuma too wen I wuz shmall. We all tot dat Marlene wuz pretty hot. Rob wuz figuring he would ack dumb so maybe she would help him wit his Japanese. Robin wuz all braggin' how all he had fo' do wuz kick back and look handsome and he could get any girl to fall in love wit him. But dem, dey all talk. Dey chase aftah practically every girl on campus. Dey wuzn't serious like me.

I knew da only way I wuz going get close to Marlene wuz to spend more time wit her. Robin had one GSR and Rob had one little poseur YSR. Quite impressive machines compared to my humble wimpy moped, I mean my RAZZ. So, dey pretty much had it all, but I had one ting dey nevah get, brains and . . . one basket. See, cuz no mattah how hod da guys wen tease me about da basket on my moped, I nevah took 'em off. I knew looked totally unstylin', non-aero, but it had its function. Wenevah Marlene had to go Star Market, she would call ME, not Rob or Robin, cuz I wuz da only one wit da basket fo' put all da groceries. So at least twice a week we would hit da sales at Longs or go shopping at da supermahket so right there dat wuz couple hours of quality time jus by ourselves. And I knew dat she wuz starting to like me cuz even aftah she got her moped fixed she would still call me up fo' go shopping.

One time, Marlene called me up and I forgot I toll Rob and Robin I wuz going shoot pool. Ho, dey wuz salty.

"I going be li'l bit late, k guys."

"You know she's just using you to get what she wants," Robin sed in his know it all voice.

"Oh, but wot if I'm not that kinda guy?"

"Not dat you fool, I tink Robin means dat she using you fo' food, not fo' da oddah ting dat you nevah going get. You's jus da grocery boy to her. You tink she digs you now, but you wait. One day, somebody wit one car going come along and take her away. Cuz one trunk can holl way more groceries dan your little basket."

Da guys only tink li'dat cuz dey guys. Guys always get hidden agendas. But girls, dey no mo' noting to hide, ah? Dey too innocent to da ways of da world. Cuz girls, I dunno, ees like dey love to form study groups cuz dey all into dat cooperation stuff, but dey no realize dat nowadays ees cutthroat man. Class curve. Everybody's in competition. Eh, maybe Rob and Robin playing da saboteur— maybe dey wants to gets togethers wit Marlene—ass why dey sed stuff li'dat. Jus fo' trip my mind.

Da seeds of doubt wuz planted, but wuz all quickly washed away later dat rainy night. Me and Marlene wuz at Star Market and we jus wen pau our shopping. Wuz storming supah hod wen we came out so we wuz standing underneath da cover. I wuz tinking wot to do, wot to do, wen all of a sudden she jus grabs my hand and says, "Let's make a break for it!" All da ride home I wuz tinking, "Wow, we held hands li'dat." And aftah we got back I dunno who wen start 'em, but wen jus happen again. We each carried one bag of groceries and we jus found our wet hands kinda gravitating toward each others, fingers locking, making dat suction sound each time we squeezed dem together. So aftah how many trips to da mahket we finally wen hook up and during da summer Marlene wanted me fo' go home wit her and meet her parents. I told her nah, shame li'dat. I wuz trying fo' convince her fo' stay wit me cuz my favorite cousin David wuz coming visit from da mainland. I could see her point though. I knew she missed her parents, but da timing wuz kinda bad. Had so much dat we had fo' do together yet. We wuz going go on da Navatek cruise, stay at Turtle Bay one weekend, and go "urf" li'dat cuz we nevah go beach all semester cuz school ah. I wuz looking forward to doing all these things so dis wuz our first real big disagreement. We wen just get together, so dis wuz da most critical stage of our relationship. Bonding time wuz essential. I remembah had dis oddah girl I used to like before, Charisse. Fo' couple months we wuz getting close, den one weekend she goes Big Island and BUYA she find boyfriend. Sick one ah. All my time invested. Tragic I tell you, tragic. Anyway, I nevah like see one repeat. Finally aftah arguing fo' little while she sed, "Fine, I'll go by myself then." Ho, dat had me tinking, tinking, tinking—dangerous ah, going by herself. Rob once told me dat on da Big Island no mo' noting fo' do. No place open at night so ass why schools ovah there get one high pregnancy rate, especially Konawaena. So I figgah Maui is pretty much booney land too, so to protect her from sex-crazed neighbor island boys, I decided to tag along and I guess, meet her folks.

Meeting Mars' parents wuzn't da horrible experience I tot wuz going be. I nevah really met a girl's parents before. Only da kine where dey give you da third degree prom night and ax you questions jus fo' make sure you not one psycho or noting. Marlene's parents wuz pretty cool. Dey took us out couple times. IHOP. Das da only cool eating place on Maui dat stays open till late according to Marlene. She sed dat high school time dey used to hang out at 7-Eleven cuz no mo' no place else open. Mento yeah. So backwards these country bumpkins. Anyway, I wuz glad I went cuz I got in good wit da parents. Usually my faddah says summah time I either gotta work or go summah school. But dat summah I nevah need do either. He wen pay for my trip cuz he really liked Marlene and I got one free vacation, nevah need rent one car, hotel, noting. Plus, I no tink I could even rent one car anyway. Twenty-five ah, cuz insurance. Da main ting is dat Marlene wuz happy. So I guess I uh . . . made out pretty good.

You know how it is wen you spend too much time wit your girlfriend, da boys start pressuring you ah. Wow, no come cruise wit us anymore. I know Rob and Robin wuz tinking dat, cuz I nevah get da call fo' go shoot pool long time. Befo', we all used to be around da same skill level ah. We jus used to shoot fo' fun at Campus Center, or Campus Cue. Now dey wuz going Brian's and dey had their own sticks too. Befo', we jus used to use da sticks ovah dea. Crooked, straight, cannot tell wuz. We heard supposed to roll da stick on da table fo' see if straight. So we used to do 'em fo' make like we knew wot we wuz doing, but still we couldn't tell one good roll from one bad roll. Now I heard dey all hardcore. Dey even enter tournaments sometimes. I remembah one time I wen comment, "Oh I heard you guys good now ah." Dey sed, "Oh, no," but I know dey jus wanted fo' hustle me.

Christmas time wuz approaching and I wanted fo' buy myself one pool stick too, but Marlene wuz kinda trowing me da hints like she wanted one diamond ring. And you know me ah, my ma and pa nevah raise no dummy you know. Right off da bat I knew she wuz hinting. Only so obvious every time we went Ala Moana or Pearlridge, we would stop and look in da jewelry store so she could look at da diamond rings and say, "Oh isn't that one nice." To me, dey all look da same. Like I sed, Christmas wuz approaching and I nevah like dish out da dough fo' one diamond. Plus, diamond indicates commitment ah. I no need buy her one diamond jus so she know dat I committed. Frick, jus say "I love you" NAHF! Cuz my theory is dat, da bigger da guy, da smaller da diamond. Scrawny guys buy their girlfriends those big ass 3/4 carat kine, cuz das da only way dey can ward off ah those unwanted admire-ers. Big humangous guys get their girlfriends those leedle manini kine diamond, cuz dey no need resort to da big diamond, guy-deterrent system. So if dat theory is true den I must be one friggin' big ass modder fucker den if I no like buy her noting.

I wonder if she goin' buy dat theory? Probably not, she probably jus goin' say I being chang. "Oh, but look Suzy, look Nicole, look Kris-T, their boyfriends got them a ring and they've only been going out three, four months." Insecure! Dat would be my retort. Ho, big word ah bu. Frick, I in college.

I decided dat buying rings wuz too difficult li'dat. Too much fo' learn. Clarity, color, and shit. Plus you figgah, hakum every jewelry store you go, always get sale. No mattah wot time of da year, no matter wot store you go, always get some kine sale. You know dey jack up da prices 100 percent and reduce 'em to half-off in their 50 percent off sale, so you end up paying da full 100 percent anyway. Dey jus say sale so you feel good wen you buy 'em. Da whole ting is one scam. Anyway, I knew one diamond going be mo' than $100. And I really wanted my pool stick. So dis wot I did. Eh, if I wuz a smurf, I'd definitely be a Brainy Smurf; my ma and pa nevah raised no dummy you know. For her Christmas present I got her one $100 gift certificate to da Jewelry Box so she could get wotevah she wanted. I wen even wrap 'em up in one big box so she had someting fo' open up Christmas day. Gotta make surprise ah. And on da card, I wen write oh we can go choose 'em together. Tell me das not romantic.

Christmas wuz good. Got plenny good stuffs. But ho, da day aftah Christmas I had fo' wake up super early in da morning cuz Marlene wanted fo' go Pearlridge. I wanted fo' rest, but I knew she wanted fo' go look around da jewelry store. Wen we got there, I knew she wuz going probably take long time, so I toll her go look little while and I going return my shoes Foot Locker fast kine before come crowded, den I going come back and we can go choose something togethers. "Ho look, get plenny earrings, pendants, maybe you can save da gift certificate and we go buy you something mo' bettah fo' our anniversary ah." Chii, I planning ahead already. Just trow in $50 mo' and no need buy her noting fo' our anniversary. No need even tink. Good ah. Anyway . . . I wuz in Foot Locker for all of two minutes wen she comes and stands by me. "So wot honey, nevah find noting," I say as I realize dat my faddah nevah tot me dat neighbor island country girls from Ha'ikū, Maui could be so slick. I try to force out a smile, but all I manage is a dopey one-eye-big look as she sticks her hand in my face and flashes me her brand-new, pre-order, Hawaiian band ring wit engraved lettering dat sed "𝕸𝖆𝖗𝖘."

"Ehhhhh, wot dat smellllll? You smell 'um?"

"Randalllll, you futt-ed?"

"Uh. No."

"Then what I smelling?"

"I dunno. Gaseous anomaly."

# my girlfriend's one star trek geek

I watch Star Trek. But you betta not tell nobody now. Frickin' shame, cuz frickin' LAME das why, ba. I ony watch cuz my girlfriend watch. Lena, she slap me weneva I make da kine Star Trek kine jokes. She so silly. Onreal how she so hard-core. Scare me how she can rememba lines from da movies even—da good of da many outweighs da good of da few, or wotevas she quotes to me wen her and her friends like go shopping, but I like go car expo. She always quoting Mista Spock—like he wuz Confucius or someting. I wonda, Mista Spock, das her relative or wot. Could be cuz he look all hapa too wit his Haole face, but wit da kine oriental eyebrow action. I dunno how Lena came so TV dependent. She grew up singing da beautiful day song wit Mista Rogers and now she quoting philosophy from Mista Spock. I wonda if her parents wen teach her anyting or if she wen jus learn eh-ryting from looking da TV?

Tonight she wen promise me dat wuz going have one good episode on *Star Trek Voyager* so I GOTTA watch. Going get da Borg again she sed. I know probably going be shitty. False advertising wuz, da suckin' previews lass time. Make like wuz going be exciting, make like wuz going have one battle, but how dey going battle, how dey going scrap, dey cannot scrap wen ony get one ship of frickin' DEAD Borg. So lame. And had da odda one, wen dey wen find da planet, da planet of da PEACEFUL Borg. Big whoop-d-doo, ba.

And I no see why she got excited befo' wen dat odda Star Trek movie came out. To me da old ones wuz mo' betta cuz Kirk wuz cool. He got all da chics. Plus, he always got fo' beef. I like da one in chree, wen he wen go beam simultaneously wit da Klingons and do da switcharoo, so da Klingons, da dummies dat dey wuz, wen go board da Enterprise jus as da ting wuz set fo' self-destruck. Dat wuz classick. These new generation guys, I dunno. Not da same. I no see why we had fo' go see da *Generations* movie on da first day. Of course wen people see us standin' in da line dey goin' tink, "Ooooh, look da poor girl, HE draggin HER fo' go see da Star Trek movie. Wot a nerd, yea?" Jus cuz I da guy. And I get glasses. Tired wuz hea her nag, so I sed, "K dens, we go," but I wen go tink ahead, and I wen go make her da kine, go buy da tickets la'dat. And you know wot wen happen?

"Can get two tickets?" she tell da girl.

"For what movie?"

And den she turns, "Eh Randall, what movie we was going see again?!!"

Oh, yeah yeah yeah, *Generations*. Can get two for *Star Trek Generations?*"

I swear Randall, he always overreacting. All I could think of was the Star Trek movie, the Star Trek movie. Could I help it if I had one momentary memory lapse? I really couldn't remember the specific name. I bet Randall shame tell his friends I watch Star Trek. I bet he wish that I was like all the other girls, the ones who watch *Beverly Hills 90210* and drool all over Brandon Walsh and Dylan McKay. I glad that Randall no play around with his sideburns like his motorcycle roommates at the dorms, all the Jason Priestly wannabees. No tell Randall, but I think Patrick Stewart is sooooo sexy. If he found out, I know the first thing he going say is, "Why you like bolo head guys fo'? And wot, you like me shave my head too so den I come all bolo head? You know all da girls dey goin' like try touch my head. I no tink you goin' like dat, eh? Odda girls touchin' my head, heh heh heh heh, you catch?" Men can be so not with it. They no realize that us women look beyond stuff like that. Who cares about Patrick Stewart's hair—it's his charisma that turns me on. Like when he says "Engage" or "Make it so, Number One," it just sounds so authoratative. Just the way he talks. Sexy. Not like Randall who stay in college but he still talking planny pidgin. He such one "blalah" I tell you.

I can kinda picture Randall being one starship captain though. Instead of saying "Engage," he would say "Goin', goin'." Even though he cannot talk like one starship captain, he get the moral character. And he has that certain charm that I found quite fascinating. He always gotta be the center of attention, but he's such one nice guy. I still remember him "trying" for make macho. We was both taking Speech 151: Personal and Public Speaking, and Randall comes up to me.

"Lena, wot dorm you stayin' at?"

"Frear."

"Oh oh oh. You guys get one TV?"

"Yeah."

"You guys get one phone?"

"Yeah."

"You guys get one phone numba?"

It sounded a little rehearsed, but I gave it to him. Just cause it was kinda corny. He likes to act all like he's "da man" in front his friends, but he can be such a sweetie. I remember I got him a white teddy bear while we were shopping at the mall. I thought he would just carry it around in the bag, but he carried it in his arm like I just won it for him at the carnival, all proud.


Usually wen me and Lena disagree, it's ony shmall kine, so no mattas. Jus so you know, fo' da record, ba, wuz ME who sed NAH to da Star Trek convention lass month. I knew wuz goin' be frickin' lame-ass wit some minor unknown female supporting character from *Deep Space Nine* as da MAIN guest celebrity. Like big whoop-d-doo. If I pay fo' 'um I like see at least one of da big chree, ba. But I wuzn't payin' fo' 'um. Lena wen pay my ticket, so couldn't grumble. Freaky those tings. It's like dey one whole separate culture wen dey go all dress up as their favorite guy wit their make-pretend tri-corders, fake phaser guns, and pointy ears made from plastic. I neva know had da kine Oriental Vulcans. I guess so cuz on *Voyager* get da Pōpolo Vulcan now, so I guess nowdays anybody can be one Vulcan. Lena wuz one of da few girls dat had at da convention. Wuz kinda pitiful seein' all da fanboys droolin' ova da *Deep Space Nine* Romulan lady, or woteva species she wuz, payin' ten bucks fo' get one autograph picture and da chance fo' talk wit her fo' all a two seconds. Get a frickin' life, ba.

Da convention wuz pau already so I couldn't figga out hakum Lena wuz ackin' all nice to me today. Maybe she jus got her latest *Outpost* newsletter and da ting wen say dat get one nodda convention comin' up? Or maybe she wuz jus bein' regular nice cuz *Voyager* wuz goin' be on. I couldn't figga out her motive. We wuz standin' in line at da McDonald's on South King and she wuz bein' all affectionate, huggin' me in da line. Make A.

"Wotchoo doin'?!"

"Why, I cannot hug you?"

"You being such one enemy of da Federation."

"You told me your Kling-on joke already."

Yea, dat wuz a dumb joke. I comin' all like one Star Trekker, Trekkie, frickin' GEEK already. I betta stop it. We wen order five Happy Meals cuz she wanted fo' get da Beanie Babies. "Happy now?" I toll her. Shame order kiddie food. Afta we wen order we sat by da window and watched all da cars pass by. Planny Integras. Townies das why. Lena wuz all talkin' about wot we wuz goin' do dis summa. I figga-ed we go Kaua'i but she threw me one curve wen all of a sudden, out of da blue, she toll me she wanted fo' go away Massachusetts, fo' one year, on da kine student exchange program.

"Fo' why?"

"I like see the world."

"Go watch da kine *National Geographic*, you like see da world," I sed grab- bin' her Beanie Baby elephant and monkey and makin' dem beef, fo' give da kine graphic illa-ma- stration. "See, Trials of Life, animals in da wild. No need go no place. I can make pan-to-mime."

*80*

"No, Randall, you know what I mean. You never wanted for broaden your experiences?"

"Yea, rememba da time I toll you we go try buy sometin' from 80% Straight."

"I serious Randall," and she had dat look in her eye, da kine I get my mind set kine look and no matta wot you say or do I not goin' change my mind kine look.

"So what? What should we do?" Dis wuz da question she axed all coy kine, but I knew she wuzn't really interested in listenin' to wot I had fo' say. Really wen she axes doze kine, broad kine, open-ended questions, she jus presentin' da illusion of choice. She really jus fishin' around and she like you guess and keep guessin' la'-dat, until you guess da answer dat she really like hea. Even though I knew wuz hopeless I figga-ed I should give some ah-guments on why not fo' go. But no matta wot I wuzn't goin' cave in like how I did wen we saw *Generations*—five times. And das wot I sed da third time we saw 'um, but dis time fo' real kine, ba. I knew she wanted me fo' say dat I wanted fo' go on dis student exchange ting too, but I no like go Massachusetts. Hawai'i and da mainland. It's like separate, ba, separate. Everytin' so diff'rent ova dea.

"But eh-rytin' so diff'rent ova dea," I wen argue.

"That's the point Randall. Maybe seeing the difference might make you see yourself a little better. You don't know what you're missing."

"No mo' plate lunch you know. No mo' Zippy's. I miss doze Meal Mobiles. You no miss those? It's a meal and it's a vehicle. Dumb, eh? I guess das why da ting wen flop. But anyway, all our friends wen dey go mainland, das da first ting dey miss you know, da food."

"No Randall, the first thing I going miss is you. I like you go come too."

See, I knew das wot she wanted. Cuz I love her, but I no like leave hea. Tings ova dea is not like tings ova hea, you know da kine. Wot if I go McDonald's, ony it's not McDonald's, it's frickin' Mickey D's ova dea, fo' some reason, I dunno why. And so I go dea and order one lah-ge saimin, one Portuguese sausage wit eggs and rice, one meejum fruit punch, and wot if dey look at me all funny kine? And I goin' be all like, "Ba, mee-jum, you know, like shmall, MEEJUM, lah-ge," like how one time I had to explain to da haole man at da Pizza Hut on University wen he neva catch on wot meejum wuz. Ony dis time goin' be diff'rent, goin' be like wuzn't ony dat ONE ting dey neva catch on, wuz like my WHOLE order. Dey goin' all look at me like "WOT IS DAT?!?" like I one new alien life form or sometin'. And I goin' be all like, "Ba, wot you lookin' me fo'?? Look da frickin' menu. Look 'um, look 'um. Ai, hakum your menu stay all fucked up?? And wotchoo mean I cannot use my McExtra cod!!!"

Really, I tink Lena watch too much Star Trek her. Das wea she get all her spirit of adventure. Me, I jus one home boy. I rememba da lass time I wen mainland people wen treat me like I wuz Mexican. And not dat get anytin' wrong wit bein' Mexican, but it jus feels weird wen people constantly remind you dat you stay diff'rent. I no like leave Hawai'i. Dis wea I grew up, dis wea I like raise my family. We wen already talk about havin' da kine one boy, and one girl, and one house, wit one rock wall, not hollow tile, or da kine white picket fence, cuz I like da permimeter be solid, ba. And not da kine Futura stone driveway, jus concrete, nahf. I always figga-ed da house wuz goin' be like Kaimukī or sometin', not Connecticut or woteva state wuz she wanted fo' go. I know once she see da mainland she not goin' like come back. She always complainin' no mo' nahtin' fo' do ova hea. Townie das why. She no appreciate ova hea, ba. You gotta tink, if all da

*82*

tourists from all around da world like come hea, den ova hea muss be one pretty good place fo' be.


I don't know how Randall can say Hawai'i is the best place to be when he really hasn't seen too many other places. One time Marriott had a cookout at Andrews Amphitheater and while some band was playing I remember me and Randall talked about what made Hawai'i special.

"Cuz," he said trying to ignore me so he could listen to the Hawaiian music.

"Cause why?"

"Cuz, cuz, cuz. Cuz we diff'rent from da mainland."

"I was thinking, but what makes us so different?"

"We get our own ways and shit," he said starting to get irritated.

"Like?"

"Why? You dunno? You Local, eh?"

"So what is Local? You think it's being born here, or the way you look, the way you act, or knowing certain things?"

Randall looked at me. "Bein' Local . . ." he started, then paused. He took one deep breath, then with his hands all extending down like one ramp, gesturing like he was surfing the tube, he said, "Bein' Local, it's one feelin', ba."

"Not a very logical answer," I said, thinking he was being evasive.

"It's bein' accepted and bein' accepting. Dea das my answer. Now we go listen to da music."

I think the only reason Randall doesn't want to go to the mainland is cause he's afraid of change. I know he not going go. He probably going say, "We go compromise den. Go Vegas." But get so many Hawai'i people in Vegas, it's like they're starting one new colony up there. For the past two years, his excuse for not wanting to go any- place has always been, "But why should I go explor- ing da ress of da world wen still get planny stuffs dat I still neva see ova hea yet?" I just don't get his connection. "Da place," he says. "Da people." Everything in general, but nothing specific. It's so intangible. He says, "It's intuitive." That just means he can't explain it.

Sometimes Randall can be such a dufas. He sooo boring sometimes. I wanna see some major cities within my lifetime. I like go clubbing more, but Randall, he so self-conscious about the way he dances.

"Wea I 'post to put my hands?"

"Never mind, just feel the music."

"But da hands is important."

"This not hula you know. Just dance."

And I don't care if people look. If he says, "Beam me outta here Scotty," on da dance floor again, I'm gonna slap him. He so dead night time. I think he's more of a day person. He likes to go hiking. He likes to learn about da history of each place. Whatevers. I hate hiking. I think I must have tan resistant genes or something cause for me there's no intermediary shades of tanning—there's only either shark-bait white, or really-embarassed-lobster red. Usually if we go out in the sun I end up being the latter.

I no care what Randall says, I think he's scared. He just so used to being part of the majority, he no can handle being one of the minority. Randall says that Local is being accepting, but I still remember how he made fun of the visiting professor he had last semester.

"Lena, dis Larsen guy, all he does is talk about himself. So typical haole."

"He looked kinda mixed, no?"

"I usin' 'haole' fo' mean foreign guy, not necessarily white dude. I dunno. Sometimes I tink mainland people talk mo' than dey know, but Local people know lot mo' than dey reveal."

"Well he does have his PhD you know, so he must know what he's talking about."

84

"I wouldn't mind if he wuz talkin' about stuff das related, but he ony tellin' us his whole life story. Would be cool if he wuz all interested in who WE wuz too and EH-rybody wuz talkin', but if he no like know us, den why should we like know him?"

"You just don't like it when somebody else is in the spotlight."

"He look at us funny kine, but look him, he wear da kine Jesus sandals, ba. Oh oh oh, and da kine we had one party afta da midterm and Jason, Mike guys, dey all bringin' can juice and stuff and he brings frickin' Dr. Pepper and Mello Yellow. Wot's up wit dat? Who drinks dat? Nobody drinks dat."

When the shoe's on the other foot, I no think Randall can handle being the haole on the mainland. I no see why he so afraid. I'm not scared. Cause we'll be together. So it'll be two of us against the world. We'll always have each other. Always. Maybe.


"Maybe," das wot I sed to end our conversation. I no like her go, but I no like go, and I know if she go and I no go she still going' go, witout me. And I know if I go I not goin' be happy and if I no go den she not goin' be happy. And I know da dumbest ting we can do is I go and she no go, den dat would be like fully mento, cuz das like frickin' opposite, but das yet one nodda option. So no matta wot option we pick, cannot win. Like one Kobayashi Maru, ba. Yuuup. Eh, I betta stop wit these allusions to da kine science fiction shows dat I no even like, ba.

Dat night we stayed and watched TV in her room. Her roommate leff. Probably fo' go watch sometin' betta in da lounge. Lena wen go bring out her leftover Happy Meal food from lunch. Da Happy Meal tasted kinda sad la'dat. McDonald's food no taste good wen da ting old.

Especially da fries. We made like one little picnic on her bed and I wuz glad dat she wuzn't pesterin' me about goin' U Mass. Neither of us wanted fo' bring up da ting again. Cuz nobody like start da fight. Why talk about it now? Why talk about 'um now wen you can talk about 'um bumbai. Das my motto. I tink we wuz both tinkin' same same, but I wen check jus fo' make sure.

"Lena, you like talk about anytin' or wot?"

"I dunno. We both have a lot to think about."

"Yuuup. Soooooo, wotchoo like do now?"

"Like DUH. Watch *Voyager*," she answered shaking her head as she sat next to me on da edge of da bed.

Da theme song from *Voyager* is not bad. But da show itself kinda sucks. No mo' nahf action, ba. Sometimes I wonda if Lena ony watches 'um cuz get dat Oriental guy on top. But I no tink he good lookin'. I tink mo' people would probably dig dat Hapa guy from *Vanishing Son*—Russell Wong. At least dat show is cool cuz he can beef. Hakum she cannot like dat show.

I wonda if Lena still tinkin' about going? She might be accepted ova dea if she go. Betta chance than me. If she go, I no like her forget me, forget us. Maybe she wuz tinking of changing her mind. Betta no argue den. Betta to jus let her convince herself outta going. She can probably tink of betta arguments fo' why she fully love me. She can break 'um down, or she can jus lump me togedda as da total package. Cuz I her eh-ryting. I cook fo' her too, ba. She cannot cook. See, so wot she goin' eat? See, so if she go, and she no can eat, den she goin' die, ba. Cuz you gotta eat, right? So you go, you die. Right dea, winnin' ah-gument. But I guess she can always eat McDonald's. And if no mo' one in her neighborhood, den should get one eventually eh, how you figga? Sup'post to get one new one openin' up like eh-ry five minutes someplace around da world la'dat. Toll you I wuzn't so good at ah-guing. I tink I betta jus let her convince herself.

Afta we wen pau grine I felt like gettin' all affectionate. Remind her of how special we wuz. Tink of da specialness of our love, da specialness of our relationship, da frickin' full-on specialness kine deals we had goin' on. I started holdin' her hand and stuff and whisperin' sweet none-of-your-businesses into her ear.

"Randall! Your hands is all greasy," she sed nudgin' me away. Lena wuz now officially givin' me da cold shoulder. I jus sat wit my hands to myself, neva like offend her wit my greasy dirty hands again. Jus waitin' fo' da next commercial to say SOMETIN'. ANYTIN' to keep Lena from leavin'. But even if she did leave. She'd come back. She'd come back. It's ony one year. We'll write. We'll both become technologically proficient and get e-mail, so we can talk eh-ryday cuz we'll be computer connekid.

From one cliffhanger shot of da cosmic cube zoomin' closer, da show cut to one nodda mo' carbonated kine cube. "Image is nothing," sed da soda slogan. Do I really want dis? Do I really need dat? I still neva know wot fo' say as commercial followed commercial afta commercial. Da show came back on and we both watched wit da air sweepin' between us. I wen look at Lena's eyes zoning at da TV screen and I wen jump wen all of a sudden she wen jump. I wen look at her. And den at da screen. Dey wen arrive. *"We are Borg. You will be assimilated into the Borg kollective. Resistance is fu-tile."* All uncertain, I wen jus stare at da TV and I found my lips moutin' their catch phrase, word fo' word—like I had known 'um all along.

My girlfriend loves to shop at da Generations depahtment at Liberty House—Pearlridge, Ala Moana, Kāhala Mall, Windward Mall. She even goes to da Liberty House in town during her lunch break at work. If you's a frequent shopper, you bound to take notice a her. She's da one . . .

# da house of liberty

who gets all da sales announcements in da mail before da ad comes out in da papah. Seems as if she's always looking fohward to da Zooper sale, Safari sale, Rainbow sale, White sale . . . Blue Tag sale . . . One Day sale . . . 12-hour sale . . . 13 minute 33 and a half second sale—starting, not now, but NOW.

who longs to buy expensive, high-quality, name-brand shoes from da LH shoe depahtment wea my friend Matt Takamine works, so he could probably geev us off, but we end up going to Payless and getting 5 pairs of shoes for $6.99, which of coss geevs her feet blisters da next day at school, jus walking from da pahking structure to Kuykendall. Three weeks later dey break and we repeat da whole process—again.

who buys her make-up from the Clinique conter, but only wen dey have their free gift offer—usually a container filled wit trial sizes of lipstick, mascara, eye shadow, lotion, and soap, which she brings home and jus keeps in her drawers, cuz she usually doesn't use dat much make-up, but still she likes to go during these special limited times, cuz she wants da free gift, jus because ees free.

who dreams of purchasing a Dooney & Bourke handbag behind da glass case in da handbag depahtment, a real Dooney & Bourke, not da faaaake $15 kine from da swap meet, cuz women can tell dat sorta ting. Eh-verytime we go to da store, we gotta set aside special visiting hours jus so she can point out to me da exack shade and style she prefers. Finally I get tie-ed of going all da time, so I get her one for our one-year anniversary. However, I failed to forsee dat now we would haff to get da matching checkbook, pocketbook, wallet, coin purse, and key chain. Wot did I start?

who tries on at least one garment from every depahtment—swimsuits, shirts, blouses, shorts, slacks, even socks muss be carefully selected and fitted insai da dressing rooms while I wait patiently outsai, looking desperately for a wall or pillar, SOMEting to lean against, so I can ress my weary shopping fatigue body in one attempt to look cool, like I wanna be shopping, like I'm enjoying myself, like I belong by all da bra and panties.

who pays for eh-vryting on top her LH charge card, and wen assed if she wants it deferred, she sez "YESSS," as if she's a member of da secret sisterhood for da shopping elite. Aftah she signs, me, being da big strong guy dat I am, get to carry all da bags from all da separate depahtments. Luckily, she always asks for a shopping bag for her final purchase so I can put all her oddah bags in da bigger bag, which I suppose does make my life a little easier.

who lets me look at da aloha shirts for approximatelee, two minutes before she goes "sigh . . ." and looks at her watch like she's anxious to go back and buy someting she had previously decided she didn't want, but apparently during those extra two minutes of tink-time had decided it wuz some item she couldn't possible live witout, or at least some item she can always, ALWAYS return later for a full refund, no questions assed, wit ony da occasional stink-eye from da sales girl who recognizes it as being in style two or three seasons ago.

Now dis might seem like a lot to endure for a guy my age, spending his most vital years being bag-boy to da almighty shopping queen. But seeing her happy, is wot makes me happy. At least, so she sez.

Normally negative twelve degrees would keep my girlfriend indoors I would tink cuz even da Mililani Town Center parking lot aftah da midnight movie is already too Icee da Bear for her. But somehow, somewhere, someplace she still get some stamina all stored away, cuz soon as I saw her face she had dat look like she wuz on a masochistic mission—to shop, till *I* drop.

# *bag lady in da big apple*

Before we leave da hotel I make sure we plan our route cuz I no like look like one Japanese tourist, but no can help wen everybody in Manhattan stay wearing black trenchcoats and I stay wearing my purple scarf, green hat, brown gloves, blue jeans, and bright, construction worker orange jacket—da kine clothes dat I know no really match, but wuz cheap sale at da Ross' by Sam's Club—I figgah no sense spend money on clothes I only going use ONE time. And even if we wuz all stylin profilin, we would still stick out, cuz every block we would all be walking-walking-walking den only us would stop, cuz we no cross da street wen da sign sez "Don't Walk," cuz wea we come from das jaywalking and can get ticket, but I guess to big city business people "Don't Walk" jus means, "Ah, no sked, chance 'em, can always sue da guy."

Snow looks all pretty wen it falls like feathers like how I seen on TV, not wen it's all flying in my face—so you can imagine why I monku wen we gotta backtrack and go back to da same store we already went, making me wondah if da first two times wuz jus reconnaissance mission or wot? And wouldn't be so bad if her objective wuz to buy stuff she actually wanted, but sometimes it seemed like she jus wanted da package . . . so she could stuff and mount 'em on her bedroom wall like trophies from her big shopping safari, bragging to all her friends about da brown papah bag she got from Bloomingdale's, da plain blue number from Macy's dat sez "Macy's," and da clear see-through sack from Ann Taylor Loft, one more thrilling version of da modest beige offering from Ann Taylor regulars. Da ting dat no make sense to me is why dey call 'em Ann Taylor Loft cuz da store wuz on da ground floor, but I guess dey call 'em Loft to make 'em sound more "lofty" cuz actually ees kinda like da clearance store, but I guess you cannot call 'em Ann Taylor Clearance Store or Ann Taylor Outlet cuz das like advertising, "Come, check out all da rejeck clothes dat all da rich people don't want."

And I no see why we even hafto look all da stores on Madison and 5th Avenue like Versace, Ferragamo, Gucci, Fendi, Bulgari, Tiffany's, and Cartier cuz I tink we get all those stores back home. At least I tink we get 'em, I no really notice cuz das da kine store we no even look 'em in da window wen we stay shopping at da mall.

*92*

Da only classy store we go wen we go Ala Moana is Neiman Marcus but das only cuz my girlfriend's shi-shi cannot come out in da regular public facilities. So she gotta use da ultra-clean, five-star, Good Housekeeping approved Neiman Marcus bachroom wit kleenex boxes and hot and cold running water. And no, I no really know why you need hot and cold running water. I no really know why anybody would need anyting in dat whole entire store, cuz ees like who in da world can afford anyting from ova dea. One plastic, jus fo' decoration, material buttahfly cost $149! You like buttahfly, jus go park, you like buttah-fly. Maybe rich people dunno cuz dey no look in da bushes, but get planny real kine outsai, and y'know at least da free one CAN FLY.

Wen we get home I no say nahting wen my girlfriend tells her story about our Last Crusade—how we stayed warm by going insai at least one store every block, and not jus anykine store, but da kine wit da revolving doors, da kine dat you gotta time 'em like Indiana Jones kine befo' you rush 'em and go insai. Cuz doze wuz da stores dat wuz usually da warmest in terms of temperature, but not necessarily temperment, cuz sometimes we would get stink looks like, "Hey, shouldn't you two be conducting your commerce at Conrad's or Dress Barn?" And dey raddah ring up da muffy hat old lady first, even though we wuz stand-ing in line ten times longer, and I would tink dat we would've gotten good service cuz aftah all I had my kalakoa visitor uniform on, but maybe rich retailers jus cannot differentiate rainbow connection tourist clothes from da kine garbage can piece-meal attire. And wen her friends ax, "Why, had planny bums or wot," she goes over quick how we heard 'em on da news dat one homeless lady died over night from overexposure to da cold. And den witout skipping one beat, she continues on wit her tales of adversity of how she had fo' WALK up da broken escalator in da "Department Store of Doom," da store dat wuz so cold, she sez, dat she jus had fo' buy, had fo' buy, one extra brand name jacket.

My faddah from Lahaina sai. Ass wot I tell my friends wen dey all ass me hakum we going Maui. "Maui?! Why you going Maui fo'?" dey all ass making faces. Nobody stay jealous. Dey say, "Mo' bettah go mainlaaaand." I tell 'em, "Cuss, at least we going someplace, bully. Going someplace is beddah than going no place." Sometimes I wish we wuz rich like Steiler Shintani guys who go like Disneyland like every oddah year and Disney World like every oddah oddah year in between. Wot's wrong wit Maui? Good Maui. Maui get Planet Hollywood now. Ass wea my Uncle Stoney guys ran into da Barbarian Bruddahs lass year wen dey went right aftah da special openings. Maybe, if da timing correck, if eh-ryting wuz all synchros, maybe me and my faddahs might bump into Bruce Willis, or dat "Sly Guy" Sylvester Stallone, or maybe even Ah-nold—da box office behemoth himself. And das like ten thousand times way mo' beddah dan da washed up has-been Barbarian Bruddahs. Wotchoo tinks, cuss?

I wen go lock pinkies wit all my non-believing, thunder stealing, so called friends of mines and I toll 'em, garans ballbaranz bully, full-on fo' sure to da infinite power kine, me

# da mayor of lahaina

and my faddahs going run into SOMEbody famous. And jus so no mo' arguments, no mo' debates, no mo' one shadow of one skepticism, fo' make 'em one full-on, full-fledge facial disgracials I going take some picture perfeck photo-graphics fo' make 'em ALL witout one doubt, proof posi-ma-tive.

At first wuz go, den no go, den go again. My maddah wen make my faddahs take one physical last month wen we wuz planning dis trip and I guess da doc toll him he bettah lay off da cigs cuz my Poppa Puff used to smoke like two packs a day and now he no smoke nahting. He get couple pills he gotta take too, but dey no like tell me wot ees fo'. My maddah wuz all worried if he could handles going on dis trip, but he sed no mattah wot he wuz going.

My maddah da one always flip-flopping. Jus like wen she drive. To moss people, one yellow light mean slow down, cuss, slow down. To my maddah, one yellow light mean stop, go-stop, ah mo beddah GO I tink so. In da end, my maddah wen decide fo' stay home save money. Gotta tink da future she sed, plus she had fo' watch my kid bruddah. So wuz jus me and my faddahs on dis plane ride.

Usually me and my faddahs no talk nahting. Not dat we hate each oddahs. Jus we no mo' nahting fo' say. My maddah da one get da motor mout, talking on and on to da endless power kine. My faddah sez her mout only good fo' complain, complain about how everyting so expensive nowadays—I dunno why, but only recently my maddah sez cannot afford da kine Kellogs Cereal Variety Packs. Get mo' bang fo' your buck she sez if we buy one big box of generic, look like, but not Cheerios and so I gotta eat 'em everyday fo' da whole month until by da end of da first week da fake Cheerios no seem so cheery anymo', but too bad so sad fo' me cuz

*96*

das all I getting, cuz das all get, and das all I going get, until I finish dat big buffo bargin size box.

My faddah sez da plane ride going take only like twenny-thirty minutes. And dis flight attendant stewardess-man is jus one rude dude, cuss. Ees like he tink I looking him wot, so he looking me why, only I not looking him wot, I looking him, I THIRSTY WEA MY DRINK, cuss. My troat stay all dehydronated. At least I practice da kine good kine mannahsrisms at my house. Cannot be rude, cuss. Wen all my friends come ova, da first ting I do is offah dem drink and someting to eat. "Ryan, Kyle, you guys like Cheerios? Now hurry up eat 'em befo' my maddah see."

Pre-soon I could see Maui and my faddah wen reach over and point out da window, "Sonny boy, look 'em look 'em, dea Māhinahina. You see Maui grandma's house?"

I get all confuse, bu's. "So if you wen grow up Māhinahina den hakum wen people ass you wea you from you always say Lahaina?"

"Cuz moss people dunno Māhinahina. If you say Honokōwai den maybe dey know, but Māhinahina, da strip is only about a mile long. You blink your eye, you pass 'um. Māhinahina, Honokōwai, Kā'anapali—das all part a Lahaina," my faddah sez pulling out one map from insai da airplane magazine. "See stay between da two rivers—da boundary go from da mountain, to da ocean," he sez pointing wit his finger.

"Aw, das jus like da ahupua'a system, yeah?" I wen go add-on, making all intellectual cuz das we wen learn last year, seven grade Hawaiiana wit Mr. Oba. Ho, I know 'em ah cuss. Badness.

We wen touch down and my face came all frown cuz my faddahs. I dunno how we wuz going make all style profile in dis sorry-sad looking blue-grey Geo, no mo' powah, junk-a-lunka rental car. I wuz hoping fo' one ultra-bad, ultra-rad, spitfire red Pontiac Sunbird convertible fo' make da kine full-on fo' sure tourist kine action, but my faddah sez coss too much, gotta save from now. Aftah we wen pass through Lahaina town, mostly had jus sugarcane. Ten thousand miles and miles of sugarcane—sugarcane and ocean. I tot wuz going have some sights fo' see and I had my camera all reddy spaghetti, but nevah have nahting fo' shoot. Sadness.

My faddah grew up in da lime green house right by da beach. I only went dea couple times wen I wuz small. I only remembah going down da beach and picking pipipi while my faddah guys wen mo' down fo' catch eel.

"You remembah da time you caught one ghost moray," my faddahs wen ass me outta da blue kine like he wuz tinking my tinkings.

"No. Who I wuz wit?"

"Cousin Rip."

"I get one Cousin Rip?"

"No wait. Das MY cousin, so das your . . . second cousin? Third cousin? I dunno, get 'em written down. Wen we go home try go ask grandma if she still get da family tree."

Den my faddah nevah say nahting again cuz I guess he wuz trying fo' figure out all da relations. Wuz quiet in da car and could only hear da sound of him chewing his nicotine gum fo' help him quit smoking. I remembah my faddah sed dis road used to be da main road befo', but ees only like two lanes, one way-one way, but befo' wuz considered part of da highway until dey wen make da join mo' insai. Finally aftah driving fo' like fo'evah and a day my faddah pulls off to da side of da road.

Could hardly tell dat da house wuz dea. Da mango tree outsai wuz all growing wild, one wall of weeds wen take ova da driveway—wuz like Maddah Nature wen eat my Maui grandma's house. She wen sell her house chree years ago fo' like million trillion dollahs or someting to some guys who wuz going build someting on top da beachfront property. Das planny money, bully. I could buy like ten thousand Richie Rich comic books wit dat. She wuz one of da lass peoples to sell. Practically along da whole stretch a road only had condo condo condos. But I tink so doze investor guys wuz experiencing da kine finiancial depletions cuz me and my faddahs could see dey nevah do nahting yet. Chree years and da house wuz still dea. Still standing. But all boddo boddos now, da windows stay all boarded up jus like da place wuz haunted.

I wen take one picture of da house fo' go show grandmas. We wen walk back across da street and my faddah wen turn da car around. I dunno why, but my faddahs wuz starting fo' get mo' and mo' walkie talkie now. Muss be da Maui air I tot. My maddah sed da fresh air wuz going be good fo' his health. He wuz all reminiscing about da mountain apple and guava dey used to go get from up da mountain, da pigs and chickens dey used to raise. Full-on E-I-E-I-O action alreddy.

Nevah get nahting fo' see on da way back. Only da same sameness. "No mo' too much cars yeah dis road," I made color commentaries.

"Ten o'clock no' mo. Ho, morning time, I hea get some planny traffic I tell you boy. Everybody work at da hotels, eh. Jus like Honolulu alreddy."

So we spent da whole day driving, driving, driving all around, driving all ova town—jus looking fo' see wea tings used to be. Me, I wuz born O'ahu so I wuzn't feeling dis kine full-on nostalgias dat my faddahs wuz feeling. "Dis used to be da hardware store. Ovah hea had da Queen Theater, and ova dea wuz Pioneer Mill Theater." Boooring. I wuz starting to wish dat my maddah and my kid bruddah all came on dis trip too cuz den maybe we could make like da kine Scooby Doo action and split up into groups—da grown-ups can go all sight-see and da kids can go play Street Fighter someplace.

"Your faddah not going always be around you know. You listening to me, Sonny boy?" my faddah wen boddah me as I wuz tinking of whether I should use Ken or Chun-Li fo' beat Bison.

"Wen we going Planet Hollywood?" I wen ass my faddahs again, as I noticed dat we wuz getting mo' farther and farther away from da ocean, away from da town, away from Planet Hollywood.

"I go take you go someplace first." All right, cliff hanger anticipation action, I tot as we wen go up da hill. But da expectation of eventual showtime excitement wen only last fo' all a two seconds, cuz we wuz alreddy practically right dea by da place he wanted fo' show me. His old school—Lahainaluna c/o '59. Dis is wea he spent da bess years of his life he sed. Wea he met my maddah in automotive class. High school sweethearts.

"Twenny-one years of happy marriage. You no can beat dat," my faddah sed all looking up to da sky. I wuz jus nodding, leaning against da car. Den all one time he wen jump on da hood and stretch his arms out. "Smell da AIR," my faddah sed making all one wit da wind. "AIR. Das life. Good ol' country life. Dis da air dat make you feeeel— FEEL ALIVE. You no feel 'um?"

"Yeah yeah yeah," I toll 'em, taking one deep breath, making all like I wuz feeling invigorated too. And den he wen go off on how school wuz so diff'rent befo' time. To go school hea he sed, dey had to milk cows and stuff and dat used to pay fo' their room and board. Wit a moo-moo hea and one moo-moo dea. Hea a moo, dea a moo, everywea a moo moo man, like big-whoop-d-doo, bu. Da gate wuz closed so wuz like so lame. And I nevah even see one cow cuss, not even ONE, bully.

*100*

On da drive back to town my faddah wen ass me wot I wanted fo' do in Lahaina. I toll 'em "I-ro-ro," like how Scooby Doo sez I dunno to Shaggy, cuz I figgah my faddah wuz tired hearing me nag wea I like go, wea I like go, cuz he knew wea I like go. He knew I wanted fo' go Planet Hollywood, and maybe if get time, Hard Rock fo' mingle wit Axl Rose, Slash guys. Befo' we got on da plane I had fo' explain to my faddah dat Hard Rock is one fancy rock-n-roll theme restaurant, not one newly discover natural geographic rock kine formation dat he nevah evah heard about befo'. He so not-hip sometimes.

"Oh I know, you wanted fo' go, wot wuz, Planet Holly-Rock, eh?" he sed making pretend dat he forgot, but saying 'em incorreckly wrong, probably not on purpose kine, but jus cuz he too old fo' remembah new stuffs cuz he getting old so his synapses stay all hammajang, so to him Planet Holly-Rock sound mo' correck cuz get dat Fred Flintstone caveman kine ring-a-ding to 'em.

We wen park along Front Street in Lahaina town. Nobody in back got mad wen he had fo' reverse and parallel park. Everyting so slow motion dis town. Da cars is slow. Da people slow. Even da tourists all stay taking their time. I can see da young guys being slow, cuz dey get like all da time in da world. Old guys, dey bettah hurry up, ees like any minute dey could die. My faddah put money in da meter jus half a block down from Planet Hollywood. Shmall kine tourist. I needed one Planet Hollywood shirt. I jus had fo' bring back one Planet Hollywood T-shirt cuz sez Maui on top. My faddahs wen suggest getting one of those chree fo' ten dollahs, el cheapo generic white shirts dat sed Maui on top wit bright neon pink and blue lettering. Sometimes, I dunno if my faddah is joking or if he really has no sense of style. I toll him we jus had fo' get da shirts from Planet Hollywood cuz wuz like da ultimate in cool. Ultra-badness, ultra-radness. Ho, going be so killah wen I wear 'em next week on da first day of school. Blow da doors off Ryan and Kyle's Bigfoot da monstah truck shirts dat dey got from da car show lass year. And ees like way mo' awesome opossum dan Shimomi's over-size *Cats* T-shirt. Anybody can get dat kine. Well, anybody who like pay seventy bucks fo' go see one stupid show and get suckered into paying one noddah twenty five bucks fo' one shirt and one noddah thirty bucks fo' da CD so dey can relive da excitement ovah and ovah again.

I couldn't relate to my faddahs jus how much I had to have 'em, and I nevah like get into da discussion on da difference between needs and wants so I jus toll my faddahs, "Mom sed can." Das all I had fo' say fo' get my faddahs to forget da chree fo' ten dollahs babies. Planet Hollywood all da way, cuss. Ultra-badical, ultra-radical. Two shirts fo' me, one for my maddah, and one fo' li'lo kid bro even though he too young fo' appreciate da coolness of it all. Wuz crowded but, so my faddah nevah go insai da restaurant, he jus bot us shirts from da front window li'dat. While he wuz all making da cash transactions, I took my camera and made one quick trip walk around insai fo' take some candid camera shots. I wen take pictures of da frozen Sylvester Stallone from *Demolition Man* hanging from da ceiling, da fake life-size plastic Predator, and da giant sword on da wall, da one Arnold wen use in one of his Conan movies. Had planny trippy stuff, but nevah get no Hollywood celebrities eating dea. Wuz kinda dahk insai, but I can tell celebrities wen I see celebrities and I nevah see no celebrities. Dis place wuz mo' like Planet Haoletourist than anyting else.

I went back outside to da front fo' go see wea my faddahs went. I tot maybe he wuz cruising, shmoozing, maybe talking stories wit some minor, major motion picture movie star, but he wuz jus waiting outside wit da bags all by himself. He got me one separate bag. He sed I gotta carry my own. I nevah care dat we nevah eat dea cuz hamburger is hamburger. Nobody going ass how wuz da food. And if dey do, jus go "ah, I dunno, not bad I guess," and make sure you say "I guess" cuz das not lying if you state dat you jus guessing.

Still had chance fo' see some stars walking around town. Cuz I know dey like go look around aftah dey pau grines. My faddahs wuz glad I nevah care if we ate dea or not cuz he saw da menu in da window and sed too much price escalation action. So he took me down to da closest McDonald's. He wen order da food while I watched da table. I held da bags in between my feet and I jus stared out da window. At least some of da Planet Hollywood wives should be all shopping around, somewhere in da town. Maria Shriver, Demi Moore, wea you guys stay?

Den out of da edge of my eyeball, I wen happen to spahk some b-buzzin swarmin' stormin' kine action. Tourists wuz all surrounding dis one Bob Marley looking guy who wuz kinda caught in da mid-jle. Looking in between all da Haole heads I could kinda sorta see dat wuzn't rastafari Bob Marley. Wuzn't even Ziggy Marley. Wuz jus one Local looking homeless guy. He wuz kinda tall and had all shaggy shag, all stay tangle and mangle, long black and silvah hair. All his bangs and bushy bush beard wen go shade his face and make him look really really dahk. But he looked pretty clean from far, like he somehow took a bath everyday kine. Only his feet wuz kinda dirty cuz he nevah get slippahs. And he had on one navy blue Local's Only t-shirt and red flower print surf shorts. Pretty stylin' his clothes, wuzn't all buss up like how you would expeck 'em fo' be.

Aftah awhiles da bummy looking guy wuz leff by his lonesome hanging around in front McDonald's. Kinda looked like he wuz playing with toys or someting I couldn't see.

"Dey should clean up dis neighborhood," I sed tilting my head toward da trippy bum guy outside as my faddahs set down da tray.

"You know who's dat, eh?," he assed me knowing I nevah know, attemping to make conversations wit me. "Das da Mayor of Lahaina."

"Linda Lingle?! Linda Lingle is really one man??!"

"No. I mean, I dunno. I mean, das not Linda Lingle."

"He one former politician?"

"No."

"Den how he got to be da mayor of Lahaina?"

"Cause. He jus ack dat way, so people call 'um dat," my faddah sed all pointing, making undahstand rubbahband wit his finger. "And he no scare away da tourists. In fack, him da numbah one tourist attraction ova hea. See, look 'um Sonny boy. Dey taking picture wit him. Fo' some reason everybody like take picture wit him. Must be he some good looking guy, no?"

While me and my faddahs wuz all grine-ing our burgers I couldn't help but stare at da mayor's face. Wen da sun struck 'em at da right angle, you could see da waves of wrinkles break on his face. His face had character, but I dunno wot wuz da secret to his box office drawing power and star appeal. During da time we wuz eating, I counted like chree diff'rent groups of tourists who took pictures wit da mayor. I can see why da second and third group wen go take pictures cuz ees like monky see, monkey do, but I dunno wot wen possess dat dummy initial first group fo' go make all picture postcard? Maybe *Maui This Week* wen go liss him in their brochures as one must-see tourist sideshow attraction?? But would would dey bill him as??? Da Mayor of Lahaina—Hawai'i's only homeless man??

No, get planny homeless mans. Unsolve mys-try, cuss. My faddahs wuz all talking about his yout again, oblivious to da inquiring minds wanna know, Scooby Dum look on my face dat screamed "Dum dum dum dum," tell me about da mayor.

"Eh, da guy work or wot?" I assed, cutting my faddahs line.

"Uhhh, I heard he used to get planny degrees—business, agriculture, law, but one day he jus wen geev 'um up and decide fo' live da way he live."

"But how he eat?"

"Das a good one. I dunno wot he do now. Maybe he go down da beach like grandma/grandpa kine catch fish. Befo' time Lahaina wuz small town. I remembah he could jus walk into any restaurant and he nevah haff to pay. Everybody knew him. Everybody knew da mayor. And den I guess wen he got tired of bacon and eggs people say dat he used to go hunt da kine pig li'dat."

"You mean he get hunting dog and da kine gun?"

"I dunno fo' sure cuz I nevah seen, but I heard he used to make da kine 'ōkolehao and soak 'em insai da bread. Den he wen up da mountain sai and feed 'em to da buta. Da pig come so drunk dat can jus walk up to 'em an cut da troat."

"Das gross. And wot, he no get sick or wot da guy?"

"K, once again, I no can say fo' sure, but da rumors wuz dat he real good wit da kine nature kine stuff. He da one wen teach Uncle Buzz and Auntie Tipsy how fo' fix 'em wen dey get hangover. He know all da traditional Hawaiian medicinal kine herb. So wen he get sick he boil da kine leaf li'dat make tea, den pau, sick go away."

"Trippy," I tot as we wen pau eat and we wen stand up fo' scram. Rocking to get da momemtum and wit both hands on his lap my faddah pushed himself up, making dat ol'people stretch kine sound effecks. My faddah muss be coming old. We wuz walking down da boulevard and I could see jus up ahead dat da mayor wuz sitting on da sidewalk in da shade taking some kalakoa objects outta one bag. I wuz walking on wen I heard one "Ayeeeee whatchoo doing hea." My faddahs all stopping back in da distance fo' to talk to somebody he knew from befo'—probably somebody from da ol' cow country. I know dat soon as we go home my faddahs probably going back look in his yearbook see who in all reincarnation dat wuz. He ehrytime forgetting people. He really getting old—I tink so sometimes he forget my name too, das why he always calling me Sonny boy.

I stood around by my faddahs fo' couple minutes jus shuffling my feet. My camera still hanging, dangling from my neck, ready fo' da kine quick draw celebrity shoot out. I twisted round and around, looking at my feet, wishing fo' one famos amos celebrity close-encounter, but real willing to settle fo' one casual corner kine meeting wit Glenn Medeiros or even dat Local girl who wuz in *Karate Kid II*, da one who wen go ring da bell. Slowly, swizzle stick swirling, twirling away from my faddahs I heard, "Eh, boy. Boy."

Da mayor couldn't have been talking to anybody else. I wuz da only boy around. I walked up closer to see wot he wanted. Maybe he wanted bus money I tot, but den I remembered no mo' bus on Maui, cuss.

"Boy," he sed again. "You one tourist or one Local?"

"Um, I guess one Local tourist."

"Das a good one," he sed smiling one perfeck toothpaste commercial smile. "We no get too much a dat around hea. Wot you bot?" he axed pointing to my package.

"Planet Hollywood T-shirts."

"Oh," he sed looking kinda disappointed. Maybe he wuz hoping I had food. I wish I nevah indigest all my hamburger. He turned his attention away from me as he looked down at someting and continued doing wot he wuz doing—drawing little squares on top da sidewalk wit da edge of one sharp stone. I nevah know whether fo' make like one Van Damme and split or stay and talk to him sa'more. I turned and saw my faddahs wuz still talking to his friend, so I figured I'd make all Magnum P.I. action and solve dis mys-try.

"So wot you get in your bag," I sed pointing wit my chin.

Den his face wen go come all lite brite as he wen turn around fo' grab his pupule purple sack from in back. All proud wit proudness he took out his collection of da kine McDonald's Happy Meal toys and he wen go slowly arrange 'em on sidewalk. "You like play chess?" he asses me as I noticed da squares he wuz drawing wuz one checkerboard pattern. He wen carefully arrange his colorful Disney toys, making sure da placement wuz all correck. Snow White wuz now one queen. Some of da dwarves wuz pawns. Captain Hook wuz da black king and I guess in dis game he wuz married to Ursula da octopus, even though dey wuz in different movies and different species. I sat down opposite da mayor, looking back at my faddahs making sure he could still see me.

"You can go first," he sed. Da mayor ended up making da first move cuz I wuz too scared. I nevah know if he wuz serious. As we played he assed me wea I wuz from and stuff. I toll 'em Honolulu. Wuz hod playing wit him cuz I kept mixing up Tigger and Winnie da Pooh—da bishop and da horsey-man.

"Which is da knight?"

"Jus remembah, Pooh is da Paniolo."

I only talked wen I had one question pertaining to da game. Felt weird wen wuz quiet, but I guess chess you not 'post to talk too much. I wuzn't sure if he wanted me fo' talk to him. I wanted to, but couldn't tink of wot to say. Took me like forevah and a day fo' tink of someting to make da conversations. "Eh, s-s-so wot you do," I assed him, not knowing wot he' wuz going say.

"I live, live life."

"Oh. But, wot you do, fo' one living?"

"I no mo' one job, if das wot you axing."

"But how you make money?"

"Sometimes I sell these Happy Meal toys. People buy you know chree dollah one. Das mo' than da meal. Onreal, no?"

"But you no work? I heard you used to get all kine choke degrees."

"I free. I not one slave to my job like da ress of da peoples. I not into accumulation of status. In fack, my money, I gave moss of 'em away. Planny people tink I homeless, but I not homeless, I get one home. And I used to get one family. Till my wife wen die young. Yuuup, I used to get one beeg family." Aftah he sed dat he jus closed his eyes, like he wuz going cry, but he nevah. Wot he wuz doing I tot, maybe he wuz going sleep I wen stay specu-ma-late, but den he starting chanting, chanting someting.

Maybe he wuz calling his chess 'aumakua or someting cuz I jus ate his Fox and da Hound. Fo' couple minutes he went off and I nevah know wot he wuz going do next. I tot of ditching him, but he opened his eyes again and continued talking sa'more.

"Everyting changing around hea, boy. I been hea while da world fought two, chree, no four wars. Every morning you can count on me being somewhere along dis strip. I no tink dis town would be da same witout me. I can tell you everyting dat happen hea in da lass seventy-six years. Da whole history of dis town stay in me."

"So wot going happen wen you die?"

*108*

"I'll still live on in oddah people's memories. You die da true death wen you are forgotten," he sed all nodding his head, agreeing wit himself.

Das wen my faddahs cot up to us and looked at us like wot we doing. Fo' one second I tot of assing my faddahs if we could take pictures wit da mayor, cuz he wuz famous and all. I looked at da mayor den I looked at my faddahs. I froze not knowing wot to do. During dat split second of indecision my decision wuz made wen my faddahs wen go tilt his head "WE GO," so I left da mayor hanging even though wuz still my turn. I wuz going geev da mayor da k-dens catch you latah shaka, but he nevah look up.

As we wuz walking away, I nevah know I wuz making all room-a-zoom-zoom Speed Buggy and I wuz all passing my faddah's pace so I wen slow 'em down so my faddahs could keep up. I noticed, he wuz all sucking, sucking, sucking wind, like he wuz on his lass breath alreddy so I wen step da brakes. I wen realize dat I leff behind my prize Planet Hollywood package. Looking over my shoulder I wen change my mind ten thousand times, I tot, geff 'em, no geff'em, go geff 'em, tinking of how pissed my faddahs wuz going be. Finally, I wen jus leave my shirt fo' da mayor fo' choose how fo' use as he saw fit. Before we wen turn da corner, I wen go snap one picture of da mayor all staring at da board so I had someting fo' da purposes of preservations. I walked on, den I looked back again fo' see if da mayor wuz going look up, but he jus continued playing, moving my pieces fo' me, as if I nevah left.

Trina's parents already all having one conniption jus cuz we NOT married. Da reason we nevah like spend da money on one wedding is cuz we wanted fo' be able fo' put da down payment on da house. And now

# da coming of kū

wit dis new addition, we going be even mo' in debt, brah.

"Vinnie, we go name him Chance if it's a boy. Or Fortuna if it's a girl," Trina sed washing da plate.

"Das dumb, brah. I like our keed have one Hawaiian name. Kū."

"Das such one violent name," Trina countered rolling her eyeballs all dramatic kine.

Sometimes I like wash instead of rinse, but she sez I bettah at stacking, cuz I da engineer. But brah, we wen study bridges and buildings, not dis kine pots and pans. I wuz four years outta school and Trina wuz six months pregnant and you would've tot dat we would've had dis conversation mo' early, but I nevah imagine dat we would be all arguing about dis.

"I no like my keed grow up be panty. Kū! I have spoken." I crossed my arms and made my eyes all intense as I tried fo' keep my face straight.

"Oh, sorrrry ah! You cannot tink one noddah name?"

"Ees a strong name."

"Why gotta be Hawaiian fo'? You, only get little bit Hawaiian. In fack, da little bit you get is questionable. You might not have any at all. Why all of a sudden you all li'dat? You wuz listening too much Sudden Rush again, ah? So wot, we gotta name him part aftah allll your nationalities? And mines too den? His name going be so goddam long. He going run outta bubbles filling out his name on top da SAT. Dey use SAT's in private school? I wondah?"


Who would've tink-ed dat our child wuz going drive one wedge between me and Trina? Can tell from da way Trina stay clanking da dishes dat she kinda upset wit me. Plus, she no like 'em cuz I so shua dat we going have one boy. I toll her we go check den, but she nevah like. She wanted fo' make surprise. We small kine beefing so I dunno how we going be all cordial tonight wen her parents come ova drink coffee and check out da baby's room. Cuz, boy I tell you, I reallllly looking forward to seeing da maddah. I know she going make cracks about my stomach like, "Oh, I see Trina's been feeding you well Vincent." Poke, poke.

Da maddah always gotta say someting. If me and Trina no come to one agreement on da names I know Mrs.-I-No-Can-Mind-My-Own-Business going interfere and make tings mo' complicated, her wit her kooky kine rules. I know she like us name 'em one long name cuz den we can cut 'em short, like how her name Cat is short for Catherine. And how she wen name Trina, Trina cuz das short for Catrina. I no see wot's da point. Short, long, no mattah. Trina still tinking how hers one going pass inspection. I no tink so da maddah going believe dat Chance is short for Chancem.

To tink, I going have one family pre-soon. Fo' long time, all I had wuz my job. I wuz single fo' how long befo' I met Trina. All da guys in my survey group all get keeds li'dat—I wuz da last one. I no tink my job going pay enough. You would tink dat wit one Civil Engineering degree da pay would be at least half-way decent. Next month I can finally take da Professional Engineering Exam, but I dunno how much raise da boss going geev me. He tell me, at least I no need go out in da field all-a-time, but I going miss cruisin' wit da boyz. Us, we pau fass every time and we go hang out at one of da new K-Marts befo' we go back to da office. We time 'um jus right so by da time we get back ees too late fo' da boss give us one noddah job fo' start. But not like get planny jobs fo' do anyway—construction slow right now in Hawai'i. And no tink we lazy. Most of da guys get two jobs cuz dey get families. Night time dey go work bartending or hotel service in Waiks. My friend jus got me one noddah job down Germaine's Lū'au, Campbell Industrial sai, working weekends, li'dat. Money going be tight.

In my single days, I remembah, I wuz too busy saving money fo' even tink about women. Nah, I dunno wot I talking, I jus talking. I only exaggerating fo' da kine dramatic emphasis. I no like mislead you—I no like you tink I wuz da kine li'dat, so of course I used to TINK about women, but wot I saying is dat my financial situation at da time nevah make 'um, uh, economically viable fo' me fo' date casual kine. In fack, I wuz bachelor fo' so long dat I noticed dat I wuz actually looking wea I going while I wuz walking 'round da stores. Befo' wuz like "Ho, check her out," instead of "Ho! Right on, get sale."

Back den saving wuz hod cuz half my paycheck wuz going out to pay da rent fo' da apartment I had in town. Dating coss money and I nevah have time fo' look. Den one day wen I wuzn't even looking, I jus had to. She wuz da waitress at da Zippy's by Wisteria. Da young one. Good looking. Tan. Short hair, but not butch. Wit da beige sweater, sleeves pulled up. Nice forearms. Can carry mo' plates than dat weakling manager guy who had to use da folding stand.

I wen jus pau work. We wen pau surveying da Kapolei lot ahead of time so da boss sed we could dig. Wuz still early. Could go beach. Should go supahmarket. Hungry. But too lazy fo' go home cook dinner. Stopped by da nearest Zippy's on my way home. I wuz checking out da menu wen I found myself not really noticing da Hawaiian Stew, Miso Chicken, and da oddah specials anymo' even though I wuz real hungry. Sat up straight and pulled down my shirt so make sure my stomach nevah stick out. At least not too much. Cuz girls really dig guys wit stomachs. Nah, I dunno. I jus talking. Das ony cuz I get belly das why. If I wuz shredded den I'd tell you da opposite. I tink wuz da side order saimin, french fry in addition to da tripe stew wit two-scoop extra rice dat wen make her comment, "Wow, you can eat all dat?"

"Why, you saying I fat?" is wot I toll her.

She gave me da bess answer I tink I evah heard, "You jus have one real healthy appetite."

She wuz nice, yeah. I wuz checking her out, but ony checking her out when she wuzn't looking so she wouldn't know dat I wuz checking her out. And I tot I saw her once checking me out, but wen I wen turn, she wen turn, so I wuzn't sure if she wuz checking me out. Den, one time, we wen both turn, and den away again, and das wen we wen discover dat we wuz both checking each oddah out, at da same time, by mistake. Wuz during dat split second dat we shared a glance dat we fell all in love. Now we wuz all living together in one house up Newtown, 'Aiea sai. Going take about thirty years fo' pay up da mortgage, but now I dunno, wot if we no lass dat long?


"Private school?! I like my boy, Kū, go to one Hawaiian immersion skool so he can learn his language."

"But you all mix up kapakahi. So wot he going be—quadralingual? My ma used to make me go Japanese school wen I wuz small and I hated it."

"Dis diff'rent."

"At least I can kinda use da Japanese cuz all da tourists. But how he going use Hawaiian? Who he going talk to?"

"Trina, wea we live?"

"Hawaii."

"Wot street we live on?"

"Hapaki."

"You know wot our street name mean?"

"No."

"And dat no make you shame?"

"Why, should it? It's probably da name of one bird or flower or someting, no?"

"No. Our street name no mo' da meaning. Ees jus Herbert in Hawaiian. Dey wen name our street aftah Herbert Horita, da real estate developer. How's dat?!"

"How you wen learn dat? Wen you had time learn Hawaiian?"

"I nevah. I read 'um insai da Hawaiian street name book. And I no like my son have da same kine disadvantage."

"Huh you! So stubborn. I dunno why I fell in love wit you."


Boy I tell you, I nevah saw her wit one face dis angry. Wen we met, she wuz all smiles. I made her laugh wen I toll her, "Wot?! WOT!!! Yeah, fo' real kine, das wot I like eat." I wuzn't going order da Tripe Stew, but chics dig it wen you eat weird shit. Mo' manly ah. Spirit of adventure. So I

114

dunno if wuz my personality, my courage, or my big body dat attracted her. Cuz I wuz making sure fo' flex my arm small kine wen I wuz holding my water. Jus so she could see my warrior band tattoo yeah. Cuz women dig tattoos. Nah. I jus talking again. I dunno. Ony cuz I get das why. If she made one face dat to me would indicate dat she wuz one non-tattoo apprecia- tor den I would jus switch and go sit da oddah side of da table so she ony can see da arm dat no mo' da tat- too. Show off my pumped bicep. BAM! Feel. Try feel. K das nahf, brah. Hands off da merchandise.

Can tell dat I on one program but, yeah? Eh, stop looking my stomach. Some guys get da kine program wea dey take protein shit cuz dey like build mass. Some guys avoid fat cuz dey like go fo cuts. Me, I on da kine program wea you jus liff, fo' say dat you liff. Small kine poseur, but so long I get da belly, nobody can say noting, cuz da belly is wot makes me look tough. But you say, "But Vinnie, not all fat guys look tough." First of all, I not FAT. Dis brah, is da kine, fatty, solid, muscle TISSUES. And ees not so much da belly dat make you look tough, but da way you wear 'um—you gotta make like you PROUD you get one belly.


"You no understand Trina," I tell her as we start drying and putting away. "Hawaiian is da host culture. We should all know some Hawaiian. It constantly surrounds us. All da place names get meaning you know. All da street names is in Hawaiian. Funny but all da places dat get da mos Hawaiians da street names not. And den da kine, get all da Hawaiian music dat we listen to. Would be so awesome if we actually knew wot da words meant, too."

"Wot about his English?"

"Wot about his english!"

"You not worried dat his English not going be so good? How he going compete wit da ress of da kids?"

"Compete? He no need compete. He jus gotta do his best. You putting too much pressure on my boy already and he not even born yet."

So much responsibility raising one keed. Wot if you no raise 'um right and he come all delinquent, he going end up joining one gang, doing drugs, shoot couple people, go jail, get out in two months fo' good behavior and den start ovah da whole ting again. I dunno how my ma wen handle raising me. Especially since my faddah leff us befo' I wuz even born. I nevah knew my faddah. My maddah nevah talked nahting about him.

No mattah wot happens I going make sure my boy know eh-ryting about me. I going tell him all da stories. "Boy, befo' you wuz born, your maddah wanted fo' call you Booboo you know. Someting li'dat."

I jus smile to myself cuz my own joke and I see Trina trying not fo' look at me. So I try not fo' look at her. She turns away. I turn away too, but wen I turn away I cannot help chuckling to myself, so finally she turn me around, "Vinnie, wot you laughing at?"

Ees funny cuz Trina's belly stay bigger than mine now. I realize dat wen I try wrap my arms around her and my hands jus barely reach. I whisper in her ear, "We not fighting, yeah? We jus talking, yeah fatty."

"Look who's talking," she pokes my stomach. "You bettah suck in your gut wen my mom comes. I know she's gonna make comments like, 'Trina's the one who's supposed to be eating for two Vincent.'"

"Wot about you?"

"I'm pregnant. And dis is not fat. Dis mus-cle."

"I used to tag. I confesss. I admit it. No shame brah, no shame," Haki said as he moved to da edge of his chair, trying not to fake his confidence. Sensing dat da admissions dude was gonna give him hassles, Haki continued on wit his proof statement. "Some people might tink of me as one vandalist—da kine delinquent of society. Das wrong. Incorreck. E-rro-ne-ous. Ees da Toys brah, da Toys. Deys da ones dat geev us graffiti artists one bad name. Frickin'

*graffiti artist*

novices, brah, novices. Amateurs! Only easy do da kine stuff dey do. Frickin' 'ōkole pukas. I hate wen dey write over our stuff. Take all a two seconds fo' write da kine stupid messages dey write—dey dunno wot da hell dey doing, spraying gang markers like BET, BHP, DOT, wotevahs, jus fo' claim their turf. And takes like no talent to write da kine un-original obscenities or da kine lovelorn, lovesick kine messages. Stuff li'dat-—das not my bag. People no realize da time das involve in my craft. Wot people dunno brah, is dat ees one art form. So das why I like try get into your guys' prestigious art program," Haki rationalized to da admissions guy who continued tapping his thumbs together witout saying a word through Haki's whole spiel. Da silence making Haki nerjous.

Haki's parents wen pay one substantial amount for his plane fare—too much was riding on dis interview. Da parents would be all disappointed if he never get in. Not to mention cousin Coco would've wanted him to go school, to be somebody. Haki's mom wanted him to go college after high school graduation. Haki said dat school wasn't his ting, but just to make da mom happy he compromised and went community college part-time and he did on-da-side-work airbrushing T-shirts at da old Ritz store and at da little stall in da back of Pearl Kai Sportscards. To Haki it wasn't creatively challenging. Everybody always wanted da same old "Candy loves Brando" in cursive letters wit blue high-lights and white sparkles or da ubiquitous fully dropped Toyota mini-truck in either sapphire blue or smoky grey. After a while da air-brush fad died down and da shops had to close, forcing Haki into early retirement.

Da parents once again urged him to go school and do someting wit his life. Actually da dad never really push dat hard cause he never went school and he turned out good. Da mom was da one who was giving Haki plenny heat. Every day da mom would say someting when Haki came back from disappointing job interviews—"Haki, no trow way your life. You get good head. You should go sa'more school, get one degree. Get into comput-ers like your second cousin Pete. I hear he making good money now. And get planny jobs on da main-land."

As job prospects looked more and more bleak, Haki thought about open-ing up his own airbrush stand, maybe in Waikīkī, painting portraits of tourists or someting, but den he thought dat dat was selling out—too commercial. Although, when Haki first started in eight grade, he found dat drawing was one easy way for make

118

money. Inside Mr. Dow's art class, all he did was copy Nagels—stylized faces of women with snow white complexions, bold fuchsia-colored lips, and deep everlasting eyes. He usually finished his projects way ahead of time so for fun he did caricatures of girls in the class. People would crowd all around and watch just to see him do da Haole makeovers and perform facial beautifications on Stacie wit her eyes so slanty and Tracie wit her color-me-cho-cho lips. He got to da point where he got so booked dat classmates started offering him cash to do theirs one first. He felt kinda funny charging, but da money could go to pay for his art supplies he rationalized to himself. Haki came real busy around Valentine's Day—all da guys figured why pay eighty bucks for send their girl-friends get glamour shots from Cover Look when dey can just pay Haki ten bucks and get one original mas-terpiece, a magnificent modern day Mona Lisa.

Haki wished his cousin Coco was around to give him advice. Haki still couldn't get over it. Was almost two years since his cousin died in da big accident. For weeks was all on da news. Planny people called his cousin one sell-out and said dat he deserved what he got. Haki tried not to listen to those people. Haki tried not to do any-thing to remind him of Coco. He pretty much gave up his extracurricular aerosol activities in favor of con-centrating on doing his T-shirts and finishing his col-lege art projects. Anything to forget da one guy he always looked up to. Coco was so young, barely in his 20s. He had yet to make his mark on da world. Even though Coco wuz like couple years older than Haki, da two a dem was still close. Only people tight with Coco knew his work.

Was da summer after Haki's freshman year in high school dat he got a job working wit his cousin at Inter-Island Auto Painting. Coco was working three jobs den cause he just got one new family dat he had to support. Haki's parents figured no sense waste money send Haki summer school cause he would probably just cut class play hookey anyway. At least Coco could teach him what it was like to work hard.

One day Haki was helping Coco masking tape da back of Vince's '64 GTO when he wen go confront his cousin.

"I heard you used to spray, ah?" Haki said casual kine, wiping da sweat from his forehead.

"Huh?" Coco said pretending he never hear.

"Y'know. Make graffiti pictures."

"Yeah. Jus surfa kine pickchas, stuff la dat," Coco said looking around at his co-workers for see who wen go make coconut wireless. He saw dat Duki had dat guilty look. He was going have to talk to Duki after.

"Go teach me." Haki upped his chin.

"Nah Haki. I only used to do 'um cause I dunno, j'like I somebody. But you, you no need. You can make a difference fo' real, man. You know how come your parents like you go school, eh?"

"Brah, school is like, waste time. Mo' bettah go Fun Fac-try."

"But you know why dey like you go, eh?"

"So I can make planny money."

"No, so you can make one difference. Man, Haki, I know already, one day you going make headlines. You going make da world beddah, not only for yourself, but for everybody. Da day going come when you going find your calling. Jus wait la dat," Coco said patting Haki on da back.

"Nah, not me. You get da talent." Nobody ever showed so much confidence in Haki before. He wondered if his cousin saw his report cards den would he still feel da same way or what? Haki was just a regular guy—what kinda difference can one regular guy make?

Coco finished blocking off da car wit newspapers and started da compressor. Haki admired how Coco did one good job no matter whose car dey was working on. Haki stepped back and admired da metallic red low-rider local-style paint job. Looked way better than da boring factory paint, Haki thought. Cousin Coco was pro at getting da colors so cherry. Haki tilted his head and looked on as his cousin did da finishing touches on top Vince's fully modified custom vehicle. Haki's eyes was intent as he watched his cousin's rock-steady hand construct each letter wit clarity, connect each segment wit conviction, until he formed da bold words "Hawaiian Built" dat made Haki wondah if you could really still say dat da car was made in Detroit.


"You too old for be still living at home," da mom reminded Haki for da millionth time. "Your faddah and I not going support you any more unless you go school. Your faddah is furious already. See, he so mad, he no like even talk."

Da faddah's face looked little surprised but he folded his arms and made his eyes extra big and nodded.

"You gotta start working, Haki. And not just at one job, but on your career. You gotta get wit da program. Maybe you can go merge your interests. Go blend art and computers. Computers is da future. You gotta tink about your future." Haki never feel like telling her again dat he wasn't interested in working with dat kine stuffs so he just smiled like he was agreeing. Eventually he kept quiet for so long dat he found dat he was nodding his head and agreeing to apply to mainland art schools.

"No forget for call, but no forget get time difference, " was da last ting Haki's mom said before he got on da plane. When he got to Oregon, he wasn't sure why he was in Oregon and how his mom even picked da schools for him to go check out. Da other two schools in Minnesota and Chicago didn't even want one interview, so dis was pretty much his last chance, he thought. After he went on da brief campus tour, he went to look for where he was supposed to go for his appointment. He followed da path and saw one mural on top da side of one of da buildings. He thought was kinda weird how da artist used planny colors to make shave-ice looking people. He looked up at da fancy-dancy looking architecture of da building—da structures all artsy-fartsy compared to da kine ugly functional stuff dat Coco used to work on when he had construction jobs.

Haki saw a big circle of guys wit black portfolios standing in one cipher. Dey was all battling, taking turns showing each other their stuff. He overheard one of dem say dat dey was all competing for one open slot. Haki made one strange face, keeping one distance from dem as he followed da portfolio people down da trail dat led to a two-story student services building where he looked for a directory to lead him to da proper department. When he got dea, da admissions dude was friendly enough—he had long dirty-grey hair, dark brown side burns, and he looked kinda hippie-ish, cruisin' around da room in his shorts and Birkenstocks. Da dude was all cool until he started going off on what type of art he enjoyed. Haki's head rocked unconsciously back and forth until finally da admisisons dude spoke again.

"So, Mr. uh, Hay-kai, do you have like a um, portfolio?" da dude asked.

"You pronounce 'em Hoc-key."

"Is that Canadian or something?" da admissions guy said laughing to himself for a while before Haki caught on to da joke.

"I get one piece book. Like spahk?" Haki asked. Taking notice of da dude's blank look Haki said, "I show you," as he rummaged through his black backpack looking for his old high school sketchbook. For a second he thought about bringing out his sample pages of airbrush designs and portfolio projects from his introductory art classes, but he showed those before and plus it wasn't da stuff dat he was most proud of. His high school piece book would have to do. Haki took out his old piece book, opened it, and turned it around for da admissions dude to inspect.

As da dude commented on some of da pieces, "Interesting use of color in this one. Nice effects with the negative space," Haki's mind wandered as he questioned again why he was dea. Haki thought about how hard his cousin Coco used to work, working so many jobs and how he always told Haki dat mo' better just have one good job. Haki remembered when Coco, his wife Val, and their kid was struggling so they lived with Haki and his family for little while in Hālawa. Even though da mom agreed to take them in, that never stop her from complaining when Coco wasn't around.

"Your cousin. Must be he get 'em from da oddah side of da family, cause our side is all hard-working people. No be lazy like him now. Dey offer him money, so why he no like take 'em? What kine lōlō ideas he get in his head? Yeah daddy," da mom looked at Haki's faddah for long time before he finally made eye-contact and nodded.

"Coco sed it's one mattah of principles. One mattah of pride."

"And so what Haki, he proud of da fact that he no more money for help pay rent, for help pay da bills? And what about Val, she hāpai again. Who going pay all da hospital!?"

Da mom was asking so many questions that Haki just couldn't answer. Eventually da yelling got so bad dat he went up to his bedroom. For long time he just stood in da middle of his room and den he just sat on da floor wit his back braced against da door and his head frozen between his knees.

"Do good on da test eh. Make me PROUD," Coco said to Haki before leaving for his newest construction job. Coco made Haki pick one last Hawaiiana flashcard outta his hard hat before he went out da door. Da category was geography, da answer was, "The military owns approximately one-fourth of this Hawaiian island." Haki said, "What is Coconut Island?" He knew he should've said O'ahu. At least he remembered to phrase it in da form of one question because Coco kept marking him off da night before. Da trick to remembering, Coco said, was dat dey only build freeways to connect da military bases and since O'ahu had planny, das why da percentage stay so high. For long time Coco just stood in da doorway, looking out at da daybreak, staring at nothing and at everything at da same time.

"Tell your mom I going work. Kay?" Coco said witout turning back. Haki was too busy sorting his index cards and putting rubber bands around 'em to notice Coco's right hand make one small kine shaka as he walked toward his dirty white pick-up truck parked on da side of da road.

Dey got da phone call late dat Friday afternoon, right before dinner when still had *Captain Planet* yet on top da TV. Haki overheard dat someting happened to Coco. All day he couldn't wait till Coco got home. He thought about how couple years back, Duki from da auto body shop wen go sneak and give him couple photos of Coco's

*124*

work from way back when. Haki kept da pictures insai his piece book for reference material. Da fat letters was kinda old school, but Haki really liked da sparkles and incorporated some of da techniques into his own renderings. He practiced for years on getting 'em down. Finally when he was ready to unleash his new signature style, he sprawled "CO2 wuz hea" in true blue interlocking technotype wit heavy metal accents underneath da bridge before Red Hill. Dat whole week he came home late and Coco asked him where he was. Haki kept telling him dat it was one surprise.

He finished his tag piece dat day after school and he was gonna take Coco down and show him on da weekend. He was gonna tell Coco how da new name paid tribute to him cause it's like CO two times or Coco da second. And how da name is clever cause can also be like carbon dioxide, friend to all plants. He was gonna tell Coco how he wanted to spread da message of environmentalism and stuff. He was gonna tell Coco dat maybe one day he could move above ground and get paid for painting on walls like dat Wyland guy.

Dat night Haki stayed home while his parents went to da hospital. Dey told him go sleep cause had school tomorrow, but Haki just left da front door open. Waiting.

As da admissions dude nodded and "mmm-ed" through da book, Haki tried to make some small talk to try and get on da good side of da admisisons dude.

"Da weather ova hea pretty nice."

Not looking up from da book, da admissions dude reciprocated, "Yeah, today the sun is out. I'll bet that the weather isn't as nice as it is in Ha-wa-yah."

Haki's face grimaced every time the guy mispronounced Hawai'i. Would be not so bad if he was at least consistent and said

'em da same wrong way every time. But each time he
somehow managed to come up with yet one nother
even worser way of getting 'em incorrect.

"By the way there son, you've got yourself an interesting accent."

"You, too." Haki rolled his eyeballs.

Not really catching da joke, da admissions guy jus tilted his head. "I
thought that all you people from Haywayah all spoke
Hay-why-an."

Brah, dis school no mo' Hawai'i club or wot, Haki tot.

"I didn't know that you guys were familiar with the English language."

"Yeah?! And I nevah know dat you guys all spoke english too—tot you
guys all spoke american or someting," Haki said as he
prayed dat da dude wasn't gonna ask him if dey all
lived in little grass shacks. "You like dat one?" Haki
asked da dude as he saw da dude staring at one of his
two-page spreads.

"It's different. I've never seen anything like it over here."

"Das da whole trippy part about graffiti, brah. Ees jus one total accceptance of all da different styles. Cuz we all can learn
from each oddahs."

"Well, I guess I personally see nothing wrong with it so long as it's not on
public property. In a way, it reminds me of rock-n-
roll. Lotta the older establishment didn't like Elvis
when he first came out. And a lotta those same con-
servative types might not appreciate this rebellious
art form of yours."

"Das da part brah, das da part dat I no can understand. Art gets so little
respeck in today's society. Da government spends all
kine outrageous money on sports stuffs like building
new stadiums and sporting arenas, but wot about da
arts? Hakum dey no put up one scrawling wall or
someting fo' us graffiti guys? We create art—ees jus
dat our canvases are transient. Maybe my picture
only going be up one or two days before somebody
come paint over 'em. Brah, jus cuz dey no show my

126

kine art in da kine high society gallery doesn't mean dat ees not art."

"I see. And just out of curiosity, did you ever get caught while creating your ART?"

"Oh oh oh. Why, if I get criminal record dat going affeck my chances of getting in?"

"No no no. By no means. I was just curious."

"Uh da kine, jus once. But we all went jail, brah."

"So if you got caught, did you still do it afterward?"

"Yeah," Haki answered half listening to da question.

"Why?"

Regaining his composure, Haki replied, "Part of it is da bombing brah, da bombing. Das da whole stealth part of tagging. Da whole rush is in not getting caught. Da oddah part is not so easy to explain. Ees jus my release, one way I can express myself."

Nodding, but not really understanding, da admissions dude continued flipping through da book reaching da end part wit da photographs of some of Haki's freeway masterpieces. "How did you manage this one?" da dude asked pointing to da piece painted on da highway overpass in Hālawa. Haki's compressed caption ran underneath dis detailed mural of da sky, da mountain, and da stream. And if you looked close enough, you could kinda make out faces inside da landscape—like was crying.

"Das da one, brah. Das da one. Das da one I got nab. Brah, DAT wuz da ultimate rush. Going to da Heavens. You jus do 'em and pray you no die. Dat night wuz so windy. In da valley ah. Wuz sooo cold. All of us wuz already all nerjous. Da wind only gave us mo' chicken skin. I wuz sked, brah. Especially wen you holding one spray can, cuz cannot grab nahting. But weird, cuz, da cold only make da metal spray can stick to your hand in one way das strangely kinda comforting. Dat piece, brah, das one of my personal favorites. Dah one, dah one, we all got together fo' protess H-3. Notice dat different parts get different shtyles. And das my part," Haki said tracing his hand over da two word title.

"What does it say," da dude asked, squinting at Haki's silver mechanical signature lettering wit blue and gold chrome effects.

"Aloha 'āina."

"What is that?"

"Love of da land. Love . . . of . . . da . . . land."

Remembering da time when dey all got arrested, Haki thought wasn't funny den but was now cause da irony. Haki and his crew went jail. But was da government who built da freeway, desecrating all da sacred sites. So instead of getting arrested for vandalism, dey should've got arrested for vandalizing da vandalism.

Haki flashbacked to his brief stay at da Pearl City station. Da chill in da cell made him wish he never wear one tank top. Da parents never even look at him through da whole time when dey went down to pick him up from jail. Dey never talk to him for quite a while afterwards. He wished dey would yell at him or something, at least den he would know dat dey still loved him. Finally, a few days later his mom asked him one question— "Why?" And Haki came all teary as he remembered da night his mom came home from da hospital wit da news of da fatal construction mishap on da freeway. He swallowed hard and answered, "For Coco. For us," and his mom jus closed her eyes and nodded.

Catching himself getting all emotional, Haki wiped his eyes with da sleeve of his shirt fast kine as da dude turned to da last page in da piece book. Da dude noticed photos taped on da inside of da back cover, photos of pieces dat Coco made. He tilted his head to da left. Then he tilted his head to da right. Then he zoomed his face in to get one real up-close look.

"Y'know what? Man, I kinda like these. These show promise. I like this surf scene. The water looks so real, like I could swim in it. I think we might be in touch, Haki."

"But, but . . ."

"No buts," da dude said grabbing Haki's hand to shake it.

As da dude shut da piece book close, Haki felt da brief breeze sweep back his bangs. He put his piece book in his backpack as da admissions dude patted him on da shoulder escorting him to da exit. Witout turning around, Haki left da room, closing da door behind him.

He felt da crisp chill of da morning air as he walked down da hallway. Stopping at da first pay phone he saw, he wondered what time it was back home. Holding da phone between his ear and shoulder, he thought of calling his parents collect before he returned to let dem know da verdict. But was it too early to tell? And would dey object to his calling? He hesitated, da phone still frozen in his hand.

De tawt hi waz wan a dem. Big Ben da bichreya. Hi wen pfe ap hiz Loko rutz, bat hi wen put daun hiz kalchrol heritej. Æfta da riilekshenz awv 2022 hiz bainæriz wen go awl balistik æn hiz programin kam awl hæmajæng. Hi wen go mek da mændeit dæt dea waz tu bi no Pijin in skul watso-evaz. Nat in da klæsrum. Nat aut awv da klæsrum. Nat æt hom. Nat iven awn da plegraun.

# pijin wawrz

Æt frs da majawriti waz awl fo it, da tingkinz waz dæt yu nid Ingglish fo bi pat awv da biga pikcha. Bat den tingz stated getin ekstrim. Milyenz awv pipol wen protes, saitin da raits tu fri spich anda da protekshen awv da kanstityushen. Da Pidgin Guerrilla æn hiz armi awv rebolz kawlin demselfs da Pidgin Protectorate wen arm demselfs wit mægnetik pals raifolz æn stawrm da State Compu-Capitol. De waz trnd bæk imidietli bai The Gates Global Consulate hu wen diklea Hawaii waz anda marshol law. Turizom waz æt wan awl taim lo kawz onli doz hu kud tawk laik da English Empire kud nau enta da steit. De sent daun chrups tu enfaws Big Ben's rulin. De waz nau evriwea. No wan kud chras nobadi. Neiba kud go agens neiba. Brada kud trn agens brada.

Waz da hart awv nait wen da gardz fainali lef fo go finish ap dea raunz. Æfta hæf-æn-áwr awv stænin stil, Jimmy shuk aut hiz armz æn legz wail Ed roteited hiz nek. Kawika waipt hiz shu awn da græs.

Schrechin samoa, Jimmy shuk hiz hed, chraiin fo get da darknes auta hiz main æn kansenchreit awn da mætaz æt hæn. Fainali, breikin da sailens, hi wisprd, "See ah boys, good ting I made us wear da kine camouflage."

"How come they never see us?" Kawika æskt bot a dem.

"Dey so use-to to da kine hi-tech cloaking technology dat nobody boddahs lookin' fo da kine body-paint and sticks and twigs up your clothes ah, y'know da kine," Jimmy sed ædmairin hiz hændi wrk.

"Jimmy, when you said for go stay make like one tree, I thought we was going LEAVE braw, I never know you meant literally go stay make like one tree and stand still for like ten hours. Hard you know, not for cough while they was all stay taking one smoke break," Kawika grambold shekin hiz hed. "And try stay like you know what was the worst part?" Kawika æskt pointin tu hiz shu.

"What? Somebody stepped on your toe?" Ed sed nat lukin æt Kawiks.

"Braw. Somebody wen go stay PISS on top my foot," Kawiks sed chraiin nat fo tawk laud.

Awlwez gramblin, Jimmy tawt. If wi kæn jas stik tu da plæn den meibi wan dei wi kæn revolushenaiz tingz araun hia. Da frs step waz getin insai dæt bildin Jimmy rimainded himself. Klæpin hiz hænz tugeda, Jimmy sed, "Kay boys, we go make like one shovel."

"So what, we can finally go stay go then?"

"No, I mean literally we go dig," Jimmy tol Kawiks jas æz hi waz abaut fo sit daun awn tap wan big rak dæt kaina lukt laik Tutu's rak bæk hom. "We gotta finish digging da hole," Jimmy sed teikin da shavol fram auta da bushez æn hændin om tu Kawiks.

Dea waz jas sailent agriment æz da boiz kantinyud digin. Bat æfta chri
awrz de stil neva ekskaveit wan hol big inaf fo ene a
dem go fit chru. Jimmy waz awl fijetin. Waz goin bi
san ap priti sun. If de neva pau da hol sun den de wud
hæf tu chro awl da drt bæk insai æn weit til neks mant
fo chrai agen. Meibi de nided wan bæk-ap plæn.
"I geff 'um," Jimmy sed kaina laud æz sadenli hiz finggaz wen signol dæt
hi hæd wan inspareishen.
"Yo man, watch the volume. The satellites are still up there," Ed wen
wawrn.
"Braw, the satellites no can hear. They only can see. We gotta stay worry
about the digi-cams," Kawika sed panchin Ed awn da
arm. "Ever since Jeremy Industries went go get the
contract, they hooked up Big Ben with the kine
cyber-optics, like that, so now he get eyes and ears all
over."
"Shaddup you two. I geff 'um," Jimmy sed linin awn hiz shavol. "We need
fo' make da kine allies la'dat ah, y'know da kine,"
Jimmy wen sei. Bat hu wi kæn go join forsez wit, hi
tawt, chraiin fo ænsr hiz oun kweschen.
Hu hæz da pawa, mæn? Ed tawt tu himself. Tu bæd Brada Joe wen go dai
awn hiz kamikaze mishen, flaiin hiz Electric Laulau hi
wen go kræsh da Compu-Capitol. Tuk deiz fo da
sikyurati forsez kam bæk awn-lain, bat æt lis hiz sækri-
fais alaud Da Pidgin Guerrilla fo get awei.
If onli Brada Bully waz aroun. Hi waz wan priti pawafol gai, Kawika nawd-
ed ripitedli æt hiz oun mentol asrshen. Brada Bully
waz taf, bra. Hi hæd da kain speshol kain pawaz.
Weneva he eit da kain poi hi wud get da kain supa
hyumen strent so hi kud lif laik ten pleit-lanch
wægenz wit wan hæn. So awv kors, hi kud jas bas om
awl if hi wanted tu, bat hi wen disaid fo prosid in wan
mo sivilaiz mæna. Hi labid awn bihæf awv awl da
indijines pipolz. Hi labid fo fandin fo da imrshen pro-
græm. Wen lukt laik Brada Bully waz geinin tu mach

*132*

saport æn da ræliz waz getin tu rædakol fo da steit, de wen go chro Brada Bully in wan pleis dæt neva giv him mana, wan pleis dæt neva get da kalo, wan pleis dæt onli hæd wawl-to-wawl awv laifles kankrit. Brada Bully keim da frs politikol priznr awv da ribelyen.

Big Ben wen den go disaid fo go ship awl da indijines pipol tu Moloka'i. In protes de wen go kapirait da Hawaiian længgwej, tingkin dæt da gavrnment waz goin hæf tu pei dem fo yuzin Hawaiian in awl da schrit æn siti neimz. Æn awl da praivet indaschriz wud hæf tu pei dem fo kæpitolaizin awn dea aloha. Haueva dæt muv wen bækfair kawz da gavrnment wen jas go cheinj awl da neimz. Wat yuzd tu bi Kapi'olani waz nau 1110100 Blvd. Æn awl da big kampaniz wen jas go haole-fai da neimz. A-lo-hei or Ma-hei-lo. Tu da korporet CEOs neva mæta kawz dæs hau de sed om enewei.

"No mo' planes go Moloka'i," Jimmy sed æz hi kantinyud shovlin da drt.

"So," Ed sed lukin awl pazol. "That means nobody can get on or off the island, so that means we best be going someplace else."

"Why, try cause you heard the Pidgin Coup was making their own computer, so you thinking the Pidgin Guerrilla stay staying over there?" Kawika wen go æsk.

"So what man, you want us to swim to Moloka'i?" Ed wen æsk pædolin in da drt. "Even if we had our boards, there ain't no way we could make it. We would probably end up being martyrs lost at sea."

"We go hijack one stealth plane," Jimmy sed pointin tu wan plein flaiin ovahed.

"And who's gonna fly it, man?"

"Whoevah's da bravest," Jimmy sed meikin hiz feis awl grim. "My uncle wuz may-jah dane-jah y'know—he wuz da famous Potagee Daredevil—Levi 'Da Spoke' Caldera."

"That's nothing, braw. My uncle was one flight attendant stewardess," Kawika sed rimemberin da pikchaz hi saw.

"So how does that make him brave?"

"He flew on top Mahalo with Captain Blaze 'Kama-kayzi' Robello. People fly only just one time like that and they come scared, so stay go try imagine, gotta fly with him every day."

"So brah, watabout you?" Jimmy sed apin hiz chin æt Ed. "You had any fearless family members?"

"My uncle was proud he was, da kine."

"Watchoo mean, da kine?"

"He was Shawn, of Shawn's Salon."

"Oh."

"Aye braw, Jimmy, if you like us stay go hijack the plane, then how come we stay digging the fence by the library?"

Jimmy wen hia rumrz awv tu arkaivis hu wen sikretli seiv sam awv der his-chriz. Wen he waz wan lito boi, Jimmy wen rimemba hiz fada gaiz telin him da hawra storiz. Da seim saientis hu wen go meik da flawresent pingk mangiz waz rispansibol fo da Glenn Miyashiro Clone Wars.

Dis waz at wan taim wen da dibeits waz awn wedr or not hæd sach wan ting æs stændrd Inggglish. Da telavijen awdiens witnest da læs of da greit dibeits laiv æz da kansol pipols waz awl yeling æt ich ada enikain. Nobodi kud kantrol da keaws antil da Pidgin Guerrilla stud ap fram hiz cher. Hi wen wawk tu da sentr awv da raund rum. Den hi lowrd hiz hed and den hi reizd hiz hænd in shaka.

Wan bai wan, pipol stapt shautin æn shavin ich ada araund. Da Pidgin Guerrilla neva luk ap antil hæd æbsolut sailens. Den hi feist forwrd æn spouk. "Standard english is one oxymoron, english by nature isn't standard. If you travel to diff'rent parts of da country, eh-rybody's english going be li'lo bit diff'rent. And if you compare english thru time, go compare Beowulf, Shakespeare, and John Grisham III, all da englishes wuz supposedly da standard of da time, but dey all so diff'rent. Dis standard ting is jus one artificial construck invented by man. Pidgin acknowledges da reality of language. In Pidgin we can look beyond correck-incorreck in terms of grammar, spelling, pronunciation, and focus on da content. Pidgin breaks down da hierarchies and instead of dismissing based on superficialities, you take da time to undahstand and get to know wea da person is coming from. We like standardize eh-ryting cuz it makes tings mo' easy fo' process, but wot would happen if we did 'em da hod way?"

Tu kauntr da Pidgin Guerrilla's æntai-gavrnment prapagænda retorik, Gates Global wen krieit wan armi aww stændrd Ingglish spikin klounz tu kanvins da pipol dæt stæn-drdaizeishen kæn bi achivd. Æz da intrnet polz start-ed tu sho dæt da Pidgin Guerrilla waz geinin in papyulæriti, da Consulate wen go disaid dæt de hæd fo teik mo dræstik mejrz. De pæst da prográmin alawng tu Big Ben dæt if pipol neva laik awpt fo go wit stændrd Ingglish, den da onli ada chois waz fo ilimineit der choisez. De wen go giv awl da Glenns da kain gun lai-dæt æn de wen go inveid pipolz' homz æn dischroi evritin dæt hæd tu du wit Pijin. De brnd awl Frank De Lima ælbomz, *Pidgin to da Maxes*, æn awl da *Bamboo Ridges*, brnin awl da brijes tu da pæs.

"If we can uncover some of the stuff, then maybe we can start our own immersion program like the Hawaiians," Ed sed waipin da swet from hiz brau.

"We gotta get rid of standardization," Jimmy sed. "Somehow. We gotta find one way."

"What we going do, if we no can go find the Pidgin Guerrilla?" Kawiks sed trnin hiz bæk, lukin araund fo sampleis fo go sit daun.

"We can hook up wit odda rebel forces around da world," Jimmy sed reizin hiz fis.

"If there are any," Ed sed pawnderin da aidia. "With American Pop culture so accepted, the world is just embracing this deals.

The Japanese practically fully converted already. Almost everyting is all in katakana loan words now."

Æz Jimmy æn Ed kantinyud der diskashen, Kawiks wen go luk fo da rak hi waz goin sit awn tap. Waz kaina fa awei so hi wen disaid fo muv da ting klosr bai Jimmy gaiz so hi kud partisipeit in da dibeits. Hi bent daun æt da niz tingkin dæt da rak waz goin bi hevi. Hi wen push da ting wit awl hiz schrent æn tu hiz srpraiz, hi wen jas flai om kapol fit, ankavrin wan priti big puka hol dæt went rait andanit da fens.

Feit mas bi awn der said, Jimmy tawt, riashurin himself dæt evreting waz stil goin akordin tu plæn. Æfta Jimmy æn Ed went anda, Kawika went in da hol bækwrdz so hi kud put da rak bæk wea wuz. Hi tol da rak tængks æz da chri chriz incht der we tu da bildinz perimetr. Sikyuriti waz priti lait kawz evri frs wrkin dei awv da mant de ran wan sistom's chek so de wen trn awf awl da alarmz. Jimmy nyu dis wen de meid da plæn, bat hau kud hi hæv ekspekted da anekspekted?

Æz de wawkt daun da koridr tu da laibæri's sentrol kætalawgin eria, da ilektrawnik bazin saunz keim mo æn mo laud, bat da noiz oni meid dem fil mo æn mo breiv æz de meid der we in bigr straidz. De gawt tu da fainol dor æn went awl wawltsin in wen sadenli da laits went awn.

"Who enters the domain of Big Ben?" wan vois wen æsk.

"Uh, dis da kine maintenance la'dat, ah," Jimmy wen sei æz he slæpt himself awn da forhed wit hiz palm, tingkin wea waz da alarm de wen mis.

"I think we stay caught, braw," Kawiks sed lukin ap æt da kold karboneit pleited kampyutr.

Big Ben awkyupaid da entaiyr wawl, ekstendin awl da we ap tu da twenni fut silinz. Wen hi tawkt, da laits awn hiz autsai pæno-lin flikrd wit ich monolitik silabol. "You are foolish to intrude. But my sensors indicate you are unarmed and therefore of no threat."

"Ain't you supposed to be at the Compu-Capitol?"

"That is just my deeeecoy. It was I who started the rumours of the lost Pidgin Archives in hopes that it would lure members of the rebellion into my clutches. You not the first to arrive tonight. Security should be arriving shortly to accompany you to your new prison facility. I have you in my laser sights. Any sudden movement will force me to terminate you."

Mai noz ichi, Kawika tawt æz hi stated givin Ed meijr kain stingk ai. Ed æn Kawika stated argyuin wit der aibawlz, bleimin ichada fo da hol dilz. Onli Jimmy rimeind kalm. Hi waz awl in aw æt hau hyumængges Big Ben waz. Ai ges wud bi priti leim if de kawl om Big Ben æn hi waz laik awl kampæk, Jimmy tawt. Hi muvd hiz aibawlz mekin awl said-ai, notin da diji-kæmz æn leizr targetin divaisez in da for kornrz awv da rum. Hi nyu dæt de wud mos disaisivli luz wan fizikol kanfranteishen. De hæd tu rilai awn pyur mentol ækyumen. If onli hæd sam we de kud auttingk da kampyutr. Bat nobodi auttingks da kampyutr. Jimmy's kanfidens wen fawltr fo wan sekn bifo it schrak him.

"Ho, Benny, wot's da deals wit standard english? Isn't dis preference on one language jus arbitrary?"

"What Jimmy stay doing? We going go kalboose and he like go try talk story," Kawika wen wispr tu Ed.

"No. Standard English is superior and is vital to productivity and functionality in the global working system."

"I think he's debating Big Ben."

"Why?" Jimmy kweschend da big kampyuta. Hiz aiz kamin awl big. "Why is english so important?"

"It is written in my programming."

"Why? How you figgah dat english is superior to Pidgin?"

"Standard English is superior because it is more intelligent."

"Why?"

"It is written in my programming."

"If das so den I hereby challenge you to one test of wit."

"I have the capability to tap into every database in the world. I have been programmed wit all the wisdom and knowledge accumulated throughout the ages. I am sorry, but you will lose."

"Ah, we chance 'um," Jimmy sed wit wan ai stil awn da leizrz, chraiin nat fo tawk wit ene saden ænimeited jeschrz. "Try listen to us talk and den we going try quiz you la'dat, kay?"

"Speaking Pidgin will not give you an advantage. I am well aware of Pidgin vocabulary and Pidgin grammatical constructs. You are foolish in this attempt."

"To achieve, we must first attempt," Ed sed sawfli tu himself, hopin dæt Jimmy fo wans nyu wat hi waz duin.

"Kay, pay attention. Eh Ed, your uncle Shawn, of Shawn's Salon, he wuz DA KINE yeah?"

"Yeah so? At least he was proud he was DA KINE."

"So wot Big Benny, you like DA KINE? You like DA KINE!!? We go DA KINE den, you like DA KINE." Jimmy sed reizin his chin, lukin difayent. "Kay, Big Benjamin, my question to you is wot is Ed's uncle proud of and wot is you and me going haff to do if we no can see eye to eye?"

Big Ben's laits flæsht fo wan moment bifo rispawndin, "It is impossible to determine based on the given information."

"No, can brah, can. So wot, you saying dat you not superior aftah all?"

"I shall process the possibilities."

Æn den dea waz sailens æz awl de kud hia waz da saun awv Big Ben's prawsesrz prawsessin. Æfta wan lawng weit, da sikyurati alarmz wen stap æn da laits went awf. Big Ben went intu slip moud, bat kud tel dæt hiz flaks hiprjraiv waz stil wrkin awn da informeishen.

"Kay boys, we go dig," Jimmy sed awl laud, rilivd de kud muv agen.

"What about Big Ben?"

"Ah, he going be tinking about dat forevah." Jimmy smaild. "Get infinite possibilities as to wot 'da kine' can be. Wuz jus one

138

trick question to get his processors caught in one endless loop."

"But how come we went know what you was stay talking?"

"Not all knowledge is found in books or based on logic. Sometimes you jus gotta use your intuition."

"Try stay like, wotchoo mean? You mean, cause of your intonation, inflection, and da non-verbal subtle nuances of the language?" Kawiks æskt lukin awl pazol.

"Nah. Pidgin brah, you jus gotta feel da meaning."

"Wow man, feel the meaning. That's pretty deep," Ed sed.

"Pretty good ah. I jus made dat up now. Not bad ah fo' public school."

"We could start one whole revolution with these Pidgin theories."

"We go try hook up wit da Pidgin Guerrilla and see wot's da next step," Jimmy sed pointin awnwrd.

To his enemies, **Lee A. Tonouchi** is da notorious "Pidgin Guerrilla," one guy dedicated to promoting da powah of Pidgin as one legitimate language and as one literature. To his friends and fans, he's jus da Mastah-Of-Comic-Disastah cuz his stories get planny humorous-kine moments, but because of da strong emotional tensions and da seriousness of da themes Lee's stories transcend da level of crack-you-up entertainment into da realm of wot can ony be called literary comedy.

*photo credit:* Tracie Akiyama